Puffin Books

THE WONDER-DOG
The Collected Children's Stories of Richard Hughes

'There was once a cat who had lost her spectacles...'

'Once there were two children out for a walk by themselves when they saw an enormous policeman...'

'There is a little boy I know who always looks very carefully in wastepaper baskets...'

Stories that begin like this mean you just have to go on reading, and you'll find that every story in this collection is just as delightfully surprising as you could wish, sometimes even deliciously alarming. The one about the white elephants who live underground and are terrorized by a magical rabbit, for instance, or the tale of the little girl who goes to live in a spider's palace in the sky – a marvellous transparent place with just one room you can't see into. You can discover an old, old queen who never dies, and a man with seven walking-sticks, one for each colour of the rainbow.

These stories by Richard Hughes, author of *A High Wind in Jamaica*, are all so different and so unexpected that it's hard to imagine a collection that could offer more entertainment and enchantment.

For seven-, eight- and nine-year-olds.

The Wonder-Dog

The Collected Children's Stories of

Richard Hughes

Illustrations by Antony Maitland

PUFFIN BOOKS

Puffin Books, Penguin Books Ltd, Harmondsworth,
Middlesex, England
Penguin Books, 625 Madison Avenue,
New York, New York 10022, U.S.A.
Penguin Books Australia Ltd, Ringwood,
Victoria, Australia
Penguin Books Canada Ltd, 2801 John Street,
Markham, Ontario, Canada L3R 1B4
Penguin Books (N.Z.) Ltd, 182-190 Wairau Road,
Auckland 10, New Zealand

First published by Chatto & Windus 1977

Published in Puffin Books 1980

Made and printed in Great Britain by
Richard Clay (The Chaucer Press) Ltd
Bungay, Suffolk

CONTENTS

THE WONDER-DOG

FOREWORD

I cannot write stories for children: none of the stories in this collection were conceived sitting faced by an unresponsive sheet of white paper, always by a live audience which had to be entertained—*or else*, for the bored child is merciless. Each story, then, began as a tale that was told: maybe to a single child tucked up safely in bed, or maybe to quite a number (the largest group I recall was an obstreperous gang of twenty on a beach-picnic, all tattooed head to foot with blue-bag; and that story was *Living in W'ales*). Each story was told moreover entirely off the cuff, a once-only performance never repeated to others.

Naturally only a few out of very many ever got written down afterwards. That had been no part of my original intention, and the very possibility was largely governed by opportunities for a play-back by the original audience. For whereas the child who has been held by a story seems capable of total recall, can tell it back next morning almost word for word, this unpremeditated kind of story-telling demands from the teller himself intense concentration on his listeners—*not* on the story bubbling up freely from his own Unconscious. The teller tends to forget his story as soon as he has told it, like the dream you forget on waking: unless he can get it dictated back to him later it is gone for good.

Almost every story in this book has been through a child's mind and back to me again like this before reaching the written page.

Essentially a performance of this sort belongs in the field of rhetoric rather than of literature (perhaps the only rhetoric ever *aimed*, on occasion, at sending its hearers to sleep). It is the function of rhetoric to reflect quite as much of the listener's mind as of the speaker's; and indeed my usual practice is to begin by asking each child present to suggest one ingredient—a character or an object, a cat, a Prime Minister or a lobster-pot—which they wish to appear in the story. Thus it will easily be seen which stories here were activated by audiences of little girls and which by boys—or by a mixed bag of both: which were listened to by middle-class children back in the days of nannies and nurseries and domestic servants, which by little wartime evacuees from city streets, which by more up-to-date children.

For this practice of unpremeditated story-telling dates back for me at least fifty years. It began in the 1920s when an ignorant young bachelor, trying to write *A High Wind in Jamaica*, found that the most intimate contacts with a wide variety of his friends' children were essential if that book was to sound the right note; and having once acquired a taste for the company of children the habit grew. Then came marriage, with ultimately five children of our own to be told stories. Then came the War, in the early weeks of which the population of the neighbourhood was doubled overnight by an influx of evacuees, and our own young family was increased by six 'unaccompanied' children from Birkenhead. . . .

These six alien mites, dumped so suddenly and randomly among total strangers on a lonely Welsh hillside utterly devoid of fish-and-chips, where there was no friendly roar of traffic to lull them but only the melancholy bleat of sheep and the cry of gulls, had somehow to be reconciled to the awful wrench from Home and Mother if they were not to cry themselves bitterly to sleep every night. The story-teller was taxed to his utmost, and it was with these evacuee children that I first recognised how often the 'ingredients' they demanded for my bed-time story recalled the symbols employed in play-therapy: how often (though quite unconsciously) in the story as told I tended to conform to cognate techniques.

Could this perhaps explain the intense concentration and satisfaction, the evident benefit received, with which a child may listen to a story however outdated and un-familiar its background? Differences of social experience are superficial, affecting at most the stage-properties of a story: its power to hold the child lies deeper, in its empathy with those deep emotional disturbances all child-hood is heir to: an empathy only communicable at the fantasy level. At any rate, when reading 'The Doll and the Mermaid' (for example), remember the perplexed and forlorn little ears which that story was first intended to comfort.

RICHARD HUGHES

Living in W'ales

Once there was a man who said he didn't like the sort of houses people lived in, so he built a model village. It was not really like a model village at all, because the houses were all big enough for real people to live in, and he went about telling people to come and Live in W'ales.

There was also living in Liverpool a little girl who was very nice. So when all the people went off with the man to live in W'ales, she went with them. But the man walked so fast that presently some of them got left behind. The ones who were left behind were the little girl, and an Alsatian dog, and a very cross old lady in a bonnet and black beads, who was all stiff, but had a nice husband, who was left behind too.

So they went along till they came to the sea; and in the sea was a whale. The little girl said, 'That was what he meant, I suppose, when he talked about living in W'ales. I expect the others are inside: or, if not, they are in another one. We had better get in this one.'

So they shouted to know if they might come in, but the whale didn't hear them. The nice husband said that if that was what living in W'ales meant, he would rather go back to Liverpool: but the horrid old lady said, 'Nonsense! I will go and whisper in its ear.'

But she was very silly, and so instead of whispering in its ear she went and tried to whisper in its blowhole. Still the whale didn't hear; so she got very cross and said, 'None of this nonsense, now! Let us in at once! I won't have it, do you hear? I simply won't stand it!' and she began to stir in his blowhole with her umbrella.

So the whale blew, like an enormous sneeze, and blew her right away up into the sky on top of the water he blew out of his hole, and she was never seen again. So then the nice husband went quietly back to Liverpool.

But the little girl went to the whale's real ear, which was very small and not a bit like his blowhole, and whispered into it, 'Please, nice whale, we would so like to come in, if we may, and live inside.' Then the whale opened his mouth, and the little girl and the Alsatian dog went in.

When they got right down inside, of course, there was no furniture. 'He was quite right,' said the little girl. 'It is certainly not a bit like living in a house.'

The only thing in there was a giant's wig that the whale had once eaten. So the little girl said, 'This will do for a door mat.' So she made it into a door mat, and the Alsatian dog went to sleep on it.

When he woke up again he started to dig holes: and of course it gave the whale most terrible pains to have holes dug by such a big dog in his inside, so he went up to the top of the water and shouted to the captain of a ship to give him a pill. On board the ship there was a cold dressed leg of mutton that the captain was tired of, so he thought, 'That will make a splendid pill to give the whale.' So he threw it to the whale, and the whale swallowed it; and when it came tobogganing down the whale's throat the Alsatian dog, who was very hungry, ate it, and stopped digging holes: and when the dog stopped digging holes the whale's pain went away. So he said 'Thank you' to the captain: 'That was an excellent pill.'

The captain was very surprised that his pill had made the whale well again so soon: he had really only done it to get rid of the cold mutton.

But the poor little girl wasn't so lucky as the Alsatian dog. *He* had a door mat to sleep on, and something to eat. But there was no bed, and the little girl couldn't sleep without a bed to sleep on possibly, and had nothing to eat, and this went on for days and days.

Meanwhile the whale began to get rather worried about them. He had swallowed them without thinking much about it; but he soon began to wonder what was happening to them, and whether they were comfortable. He knew nothing at all about little girls. He thought she would probably want something to eat by now, but he didn't know at all what. So he tried to talk down into his own inside, to ask her. But that is very difficult: at any rate *he* couldn't do it. The words all came out instead of going in.

So he swam off to the tropics, where he knew a parrot,

and asked him what to do. The parrot said it was quite simple, and flew off to an island where there was a big snake. He bit off its head and bit off its tail, and then flew back to the whale with the rest of it. He put most of the snake down the whale's throat, so that one end just came up out of its mouth.

'There,' he said, 'now you have got a speaking tube. You speak into one end of the snake, and the words will go down it inside you.'

So the whale said 'Hallo' into one end of the snake, and the little girl heard 'Hallo' come out of the other. 'What do you want?' said the whale. 'I want something to eat,' said the little girl. The whale told the parrot, 'She wants something to eat. What do little girls eat?'

'Little girls eat rice pudding,' said the parrot. He had one, in a big glass bowl: so he poured it down the snake too, and it came down the other end and the little girl ate it.

When she had eaten it she caught hold of her end of the snake, and called 'Hallo!' up it.

'Hallo!' said the whale.

'May I have a bed?' said the little girl.

'She wants a bed,' the whale said to the parrot.

'You go to Harrod's for that,' said the parrot, 'which is the biggest shop in London,' and flew away.

When the whale got to Harrod's, he went inside. One of the shopwalkers came up to him and said, 'What can I do for *you*, please?' which sounded very silly.

'I want a bed,' said the whale.

'Mr. Binks, BEDS!' The shopwalker called out very loud, and then ran away. He was terribly frightened, because there had never been a whale in the shop before.

Mr. Binks The Bed Man came up and looked rather worried.

'I don't know that we have got a bed that will exactly fit you, sir,' he said.

'Why not, silly?' said the whale. 'I only want an ordinary one.'

'Yes, sir,' said the Bed Man, 'but it will have to be rather a large ordinary one, won't it?'

'Of course not, silly,' said the whale. 'On the contrary, it will have to be rather a small one.'

He saw a very nice little one standing in a corner.

'I think that one will just about fit me,' he said.

'You can have it if you like,' said the Bed Man. 'But I think it's you who are the silly to think a little bed like that will fit you!'

'I want it to fit me *inside*, of course,' said the whale, 'not *outside*!—Push!' and he opened his mouth.

So they all came and pushed, and sure enough it just did fit him. Then he ate all the pillows and blankets he could find, which was far more than was needed really, and when it all got down inside, the little girl made the bed and went to sleep on it.

So the whale went back to the sea. Now that the little girl and the Alsatian dog both had had something to eat and somewhere to sleep, they said:

'The man was right; it really is much more fun living in W'ales than living in houses.'

So they stayed on.

P.S.—The parrot went on feeding them, not always on rice pudding.

The Dark Child

In a big house at one end of a village there used to live a very large family. There were so many children that it was very lucky it was a big house. Now the curious thing was that all these children were fair as fair could be, except one; and he wasn't just dark, he was black.

He wasn't just black like a Negro, either: he was much blacker than that; he was black in the same way the night is: in fact, he was so black that anyone anywhere near him could hardly see anything. Just as a lamp gives out light, he gave out dark—and his name was Joey.

One morning poor Joey came into the nursery where all his brothers and sisters were playing.

'Oh, Joey, dear, *please* go away. We can't see to play,' they all said together.

So, very sad, poor Joey went downstairs and into the library, where his father sat reading his paper.

'Hallo!' said his father without looking up. 'Dark morning, what? Hardly see to read!'

Then he looked round and saw Joey.

'That you, my boy? Run away now, like a good little chap. Father's busy.'

So, sadder still, Joey went out into the garden. It was a lovely sunny morning, and he wandered down to the fruit garden and stopped to think. Presently he heard the gardener's voice:

'Now then, Master Joey, how do you think my peaches is ever going to ripen, if you stand there keeping the sun off them?'

Poor Joey began to cry quietly to himself. 'The only thing to do,' he thought, 'is to run away; I see that.'

So he ran away, all down the village. But before he got to the far end, a nice brown spaniel came out of a garden to see why it was so dark outside: and just then, too, a motor came along. When he got into Joey's dark the driver couldn't see the dog, and ran over it; but he didn't kill it, he only hurt one of its legs.

When the motor had gone on, Joey went out and picked up the dog, and carried it to its house.

'That was *my* fault,' he thought, 'for making the dark.'

Someone opened the door and, very surprised, took the dog in, and Joey went away. But while this was happening, a little girl who lived in the house looked out of the window. She was astonished to see that it was almost night in the garden below, but she could just see something black moving about in the middle of it.

'I must go and see what that is,' she said; 'and I mustn't forget my magic grain of rice.'

So she took a very secret matchbox that she kept hidden behind the clock, and opened it: and inside there was nothing but a single grain of rice. This she took out and put in her mouth, just inside her underlip, between that and her teeth, so that anything she said would have to come out over the magic grain of rice. The advantage of this was that whatever the little girl tried to say, only the truth could come out over the grain of rice; and that happened even if it was something the little girl didn't herself know. If you asked her a question about something she had never heard of, even, if she had the grain of rice inside her lip she always gave the right answer.

She had often found it useful in school.

So she followed Joey down the road (though keeping outside his dark herself) and into a field. There he stopped, and she spoke to him.

What she tried to say was, 'Who are you, black boy, that make such a dark? I *am* frightened of you': but what came out (because of the grain of rice) was, '*Poor* Joey! I *am* sorry for you!'

When he heard himself spoken to like that, of course he was ever so pleased.

'How do you know who I am?' he asked. 'I have never been down the village before, because I didn't want people to know about me.'

The little girl tried to answer, 'I don't know,' but what she actually said was, 'Of course I know!'

'Then can you help me?' asked Joey. 'Can you tell me what to do so as not to be so dark?'

The little girl tried to say, 'I'm afraid I can't,' but what she *did* say was, 'Of course I can! Try standing on your hands instead of your feet.'

'I don't know how,' said Joey: so she helped him stand on his hands against a haystack. The change was sudden and wonderful: for no sooner did he stand on his hands than he shone as bright as a motor lamp: but when he stood on his feet again he gave out as much dark as before.

'I don't know that this is going to be much better,' said Joey; 'but at least it's a change. I *wish* I could be just ordinary!'

'You can't be that just yet,' said the little girl.

'Well, thank you very much for the change, anyway,' said Joey.

She stayed and talked to him in the field all day, while he practised standing on his hands, till by the evening he could walk about on them quite as easily as on his feet.

'I think I'll try going home again now,' he said, and said good-bye.

You may imagine how surprised all the village were, to look out of their windows and see a little boy walking up the street on his hands, and shining so bright he lit up the whole place. When he got back home, his father and mother were even more surprised than the villagers had been, and very glad to see him.

But poor Joey's life wasn't any happier. Before, everyone had told him to go away. Now, everyone called to him to come. In fact, the electric light had gone wrong and they found him very useful.

'Joey, dear,' said his mother, 'just walk upstairs in front of me on your hands, will you? I want to fetch a book.' And so it went on till grown-up dinner time, when, instead of sending him to bed as usual, they said: 'Joey, dear, *would* you mind standing in the middle of the table on your hands all dinner time? You will light it up so nicely.'

At that Joey got very cross, and rushed out of the house on his feet darkly.

When he got to the street—'*This* is a new idea!' he said to himself, and started turning cartwheels up the street. Certainly the effect was surprising; for when he was one way up in his cartwheel he was dark, and when he was the other way up he was bright, so he went flashing along the road and flashing through the village, and flashing past the village policeman (who nearly fell down with astonishment), and flashing up to the little girl's house, and flashing into the kitchen. He went on turning cartwheels three times round the kitchen, even. Meanwhile, the cook was mixing a Christmas pudding, and being, like many other cooks, a very sensible woman, she saw at once what was needed. She fetched a fresh basin, a very big one, and then she seized Joey, while he was still cartwheeling, and popped him in it. Immediately she began to stir, with a big wooden spoon; and she mixed the dark and the light so thoroughly together that presently he got out of the bowl just ordinary.

The little girl had already gone to bed; but anyhow I don't suppose she would have been interested in him any more now he was ordinary. In fact, he never in all his life saw her again.

But his parents were; and when he went home, and his father and mother and brothers and sisters found he was now quite ordinary, and there was nothing by which you could possibly tell him from any other child, they were pleased as pleased as pleased, and often used to tell each other how clever of him it was.

The Gardener and the White Elephants

THERE was once a gardener who had to look after such a big garden that he had to get up at one in the morning, and didn't get to bed till twelve at night. In fact, he only got one hour's sleep each night. And working so hard made him get thin and old and rheumaticky and lame long before he should.

One day he planted out a beautiful bed of sweet peas: but when he came in the morning something had been and eaten them up.

'Slugs!' said the gardener; and when he planted out a fresh bed he made slug traps out of orange peel and set them among the sweet peas. But when he came in the morning the sweet peas were all eaten up, but the slug traps weren't touched.

'Then it isn't slugs,' he said; 'I wonder what it is? There is only one thing to do: tonight I must miss my only hour of sleep and sit up and watch.'

So at twelve o'clock he went and sat by the sweet-pea bed to watch. And he got sleepier and sleepier, till at last, when it was just a quarter to one, he couldn't keep awake and fell fast asleep; and when he woke up all his sweet peas had been eaten again.

So the next night he went to watch again, and this time took with him his fountain pen; and each time he was just going to fall asleep he gave himself a jab with the nib and woke himself up again. And at five to one, what should he see but a very old rabbit, so old that its fur was all coming off, and its whiskers had turned white, and it hobbled as much as he did. But although it was so old, in a twinkling of an eye it had gobbled up all his sweet peas, and was hobbling away. Then the gardener got up and tried to chase it: but though the rabbit limped he limped too, and, though they both went so slowly, he couldn't quite catch it: but they hobbled and hobbled till they reached the rose garden; and when they got there the rabbit nibbled a rose leaf, and no sooner did it do that than all of a sudden it became a gay young rabbit again and galloped away at ever such a pace, while the poor old gardener was left rubbing his eyes.

'Well, well,' he said: 'well, well, well!'

So the third night he went to watch again, and again he kept awake by jabbing himself with his fountain pen, and again the rabbit came, old now as it had been before it ate the rose leaf. It gobbled up the little sweet-pea seedlings, and the gardener chased it: but though he went as fast as he could it was still ahead of him when they got to the rose garden. Then the rabbit nibbled a rose leaf, and quick as lightning it was galloping away. But this time the gardener ate a rose leaf too, and in a moment he was turned into a strong young man, and chased the rabbit as fast as ever he could. This time the rabbit couldn't get quite away, but it was still ahead when it reached its hole. The rabbit dived into the hole, and the gardener dived in after it, and the rabbit burrowed and the gardener burrowed, but still he couldn't quite catch it nor the rabbit quite get away—no, not though it dug like mad. Then, all of a sudden, the rabbit dug its way through into a great black pit, and the gardener, following close behind, suddenly found himself falling head over heels. But he didn't have very far to fall: only, when he sat up, the rabbit was nowhere to be seen.

It was quite dark, but all the same he could just make out some huge white shapes. So he struck a match to see what it was, and found he was among twenty or thirty white elephants, all sleeping on the ground. Then one of them woke up, and asked him who he was, and what he was doing.

'I came in chasing that rabbit,' said the gardener. The white elephant looked most shocked.

'What!' he said. 'You were chasing our terrible Lord and Master, the Rabbit Whom None Dares Disobey?'

'Indeed I was,' said the gardener. 'But do you mean to say all you great white elephants are the slaves of one silly old rabbit?'

'Of course we are,' said the white elephant.

'And you do what he tells you?' asked the gardener.

'Of course we do,' said the white elephant.

'But supposing you didn't?' said the gardener. 'What would happen?'

'I don't know,' said the elephant; 'no one has ever dared to try.'

'Then try!' said the gardener. 'Nothing will happen! Do something disobedient and see!'

'But what is there disobedient we can do?' said the white elephant.

'Is there a way out of this cave?' asked the gardener.

'Yes, there is,' said the elephant. 'But the terrible rabbit has told us not to go out.'

'Then come out!' said the gardener. 'Show me the way, and we will all go out together.'

So the first white elephant woke up the others and explained the idea to them. Then they all began to go up the tunnel that led out of the cave together. But they hadn't gone far when they found the rabbit blocking their way.

'Go back!' said the rabbit, and all the elephants were ready to turn round and do what they were told. But the gardener called out, 'I'm not afraid of you! You're only a silly old rabbit!'

'Oh, I am, am I?' said the rabbit in a most wicked voice, and before their very eyes he began to swell and grow, and his teeth grew sharp as a tiger's, and his eyes flashed fire. Then he sprang at the first elephant with a savage growl, and plunged his teeth in its trunk.

'That's what comes of disobeying ME!' he said.

But the gardener was not afraid, and, big and fierce although the rabbit had become, he sprang at it and seized it by the throat, and then began the most terrible fight between the gardener and the rabbit. Sometimes the gardener got the best and held the rabbit down on the ground, and sometimes the rabbit got the best and tried to bite the gardener's throat. But at last the gardener won, and managed to strangle the rabbit till it was quite dead; and then the other white elephants marched on up the tunnel till they reached the open air.

'Now, will you be my white elephants?' asked the gardener.

'We will, of course, we will,' sang the white elephants all together.

Now that he had all these white elephants the gardener, of course, was rich, and didn't have to work in the garden any more. Instead he had a small but comfortable house for himself, and a perfectly enormous stable for all the white elephants: and there they lived happily together for ever after: and this was the strange thing, that though when the rabbit had eaten the rose leaf it had only made him young for one night, when the gardener ate his it made him young for ever, so that he never grew old again at all.

The Man with a Green Face

ONCE there was a man who had a green face, which wasn't just green, but shone in the dark like a green lamp. So, to make a living, he joined a circus, and nearly all the people in the world paid twopence each to be allowed to see him. But the man the circus belonged to was very horrid, and made the man with the green face very unhappy. The man with the green face was really very ashamed of looking so funny, and hated all the people coming and staring at him, especially because the circus man kept all the twopences, and only gave him just enough food to stop his face losing its green.

The cleverest but one of all the animals in the circus was the elephant, and he hated the circus man too, and hated having to do silly tricks, which weren't really a bit elephantish, but only stupid. So he and the man with the green face were great friends, and used to tell each other their troubles. But the cleverest of all the animals, cleverer even than the elephant, was a mouse; and the horrid circus man was kind to it, because it used to creep about and hide, and tell tales to him about all the other animals, whenever they did anything naughty.

One day the elephant and the man with the green face plotted to run away. But the mouse heard them, and went away and told the horrid man. So he came and locked them both up. He locked up the elephant in a big barn, and shut the man in one of the tents.

The more the elephant thought about being locked up, the crosser he got, and when he got cross he began to push about, till presently he pushed the barn right down flat. Then he went on till he came to the tent where the man with the green face was shut up, and pushed that down, too; and the man got out and climbed on the elephant's back, and they ran away.

They ran and they ran till they came to a level-crossing, and there the elephant stopped to think. He had his front feet one side of the railway lines and his hind feet the other: and he was the biggest elephant in the world. It was night-time now, and quite dark. While he was thinking, a train came along. All the engine driver could see was the man's green face, which looked like a green lamp; and on railways a green lamp means 'go on', just as a red one means 'stop'. So he went on, and the train ran right under the elephant. When he found he was going under an elephant, the engine driver was so frightened that he fell off the train.

Then the elephant stopped thinking. He looked at the engine driver and said: 'You'd better come with us.' So the engine driver climbed up on to the elephant's back and drove him instead.

But the train just went on. It went on and oner and oner, till it came to the end of the railway lines. But it still went on, oner, and oner, till it came to the circus, and ran right through it, knocking down most of the tents and waking up the horrid man. But he didn't wake up in time to see it was a train that had got loose that was doing it, for the train went on and left the circus behind. The horrid man said, 'There's that nasty elephant got loose and going racketing around. Mouse, go and tell me what he is doing.'

So the mouse went to look, and came back and said, 'The elephant and the man with the green face have both run right away!'

'Drat them!' said the horrid man. 'We will have to go and chase them.'

So the horrid man and the mouse started off, and on the way they found an old man breaking stones.

'Kind sir, kind sir,' he said, 'help me break these stones.'

'I'll be blowed if I will,' said the horrid man.

And he was. A big puff of wind came and blew him thirty miles. There he saw another old man breaking stones.

'Kind sir, kind sir, help me break these stones.'

'May my neck be stretched if I will,' said the horrid man.

'And so it shall be,' said the old man; 'and you shall be spotted, too.' And he turned him into a giraffe, with a neck as tall as a tree.

So the mouse climbed up it and sat between his ears, and they went on till they caught up the elephant and the man with the green face and the engine driver.

'They won't know who I am,' thought the horrid man, 'now that I look like a giraffe.'

So he went up and spoke to them.

'I'm a giraffe,' he said. 'I've just run away from that horrid circus.'

'Then you'd better come along with us,' said the elephant.

So they all went on together till they came to an orange tree. Then the giraffe reached up his neck, and picked one of the oranges. But they were magic oranges. When he took one bite, his head turned back into the horrid man's head, on the end of the giraffe's neck. Then he took another bite, and his neck shortened, till at last it was only the horrid man's neck, on the giraffe's body.

'Look!' cried the elephant. 'It's not the giraffe at all—it's the horrid man!' And he reached out his trunk and snatched away the magic orange and threw it into a river.

Then the horrid man reached up and tried to pick another orange. But his neck was too short now, and all the oranges were too high up. So he had to stay as he was, with a man's head and a giraffe's body.

Then the elephant and the engine driver said, 'What shall we do to punish him?'

'I know,' said the man with the green face. 'Let's start a circus ourselves, and show *him*!'

So they did. And everybody came to see him, and paid a whole shilling each; and they kept him in a cage. There were soon so many shillings that the man with the green face and the elephant and the engine driver got very rich indeed, and were ever so happy.

But they had never seen the mouse. He crept quietly away, and went off and made his living in other ways.

Telephone Travel

Tʜᴇʀᴇ was once a little girl who lived in a tall and not very pleasant house. She was rather a small little girl, being only five years old: and the step-parents with whom she lived were stern and cold to her: they seldom did anything that she liked, or took any trouble to amuse her, so she did not dote on them very much.

She had few toys, and those she had were generally kept locked up in a cupboard: and there was only one thing she could do that was really fun. Some of her step-parents' friends, who were sorry for her, would sometimes ring up on the telephone: then, if she was able to get to the telephone and answer it before anyone else, she would slip quietly down the wire to their house and spend the day with them. (It is true most children can't do this, but she could.) When evening came they would ring up her house again, and she would slip quietly back along the wire the way she had come, and no one ever knew.

One morning, when she was feeling particularly bored, the telephone bell rang; she rushed to answer it, and without even stopping to ask who it was she rushed down the wire. But a dreadful thing had happened; these were not friends of her step-parents at all, but total strangers who had been given a wrong number. You can imagine how surprised they were when she shot out of the receiver, bumped against their ears, and then tumbled on to the floor: they could hardly believe their eyes, and kept on saying 'My Gracious'.

'You had better stop saying "My Gracious" and send me home. Ring up our house again.'

'But we can't,' said the people. 'We don't know the number: we only got put on to it by mistake. Don't *you* know it?'

But the little girl was too small to know what her own telephone number was. She didn't even know what her step-parents' name was either, so they couldn't look it up in the book.

'Well, there is only one thing to be done,' said the little girl, 'I shall have to stop here and live with you.'

Then she took a look round the room where she found herself. It was the drawing-room, a nice, large, sunny room—probably the best in the house.

'I think,' said the little girl, 'this room would make a lovely nursery. So if you will kindly take this silly, goldy sort of furniture out of it and put in a proper solid sort of table one can jump on and a few dolls' houses and things, I shall be fairly comfortable.'

(This was the way she would have *liked* to have talked to her step-parents, if she had dared: and as these people weren't them it seemed rather a good chance to try what it felt like.)

So the people took out all the drawing-room furniture and put it in one of the attics and lived up there as best they could, and gave the little girl the large sunny room for a nursery.

That was all right for a bit; but presently she got to know some other children, and then she began to find even this lovely nursery rather small. At any rate, you can't play hide-and-seek comfortably in just one room. So she asked the people to clear out some of the other rooms too, and wisely advised them to put away all their china ornaments in case they got broken.

Soon she had the whole house to play in except the one attic, which she kindly let the people keep.

But presently it got towards Guy Fawkes Day; and, of course, she wanted to have fireworks. But, as it was rather cold, she asked the people if they would mind taking the roof off the house. 'Then,' she said, 'I can stay in the house and let off rockets; I think it would be rather windy in the garden.'

So the people got hammers and started banging away at the inside of their roof, trying to get it off. Soon they had made a quite fair-sized hole.

Of course the neighbours were very much surprised, and asked them what on earth they were doing. So the people told them, and said it was so that the little girl who lived with them could let off rockets without having to go out in the draughty garden.

'You see,' they said, 'she *asked* us to do it; so we must,

mustn't we? After all, it's the children who matter, not the grown-ups! One must always do anything one can to make children happy, mustn't one?'

So they went on making their hole larger, and the neighbours were rather sorry for them.

But presently one of the neighbours had a good idea. He came round to the house and told the little girl he had a present for her.

'I hope it's a nice one,' said the little girl: 'I really don't want the trouble of saying "Thank you" if it is nothing much.'

'It's a sixpenny rocket,' said the neighbour.

'Mmmmm,' said the little girl. 'That isn't worth a whole "Thank you", it's worth about half.' So she just said, 'Than',' without the ' 'k you.'

However, at last Guy Fawkes Day came, and the little girl sat indoors letting fireworks off into the sky, as they had got practically all the roof off by this time—much more than was necessary.

Then, finally, she thought she would let off the sixpenny rocket that the neighbour had given her.

'This stick is rather heavy, but I suppose it will have to do,' she said, rather crossly, as she fastened the rocket to the people's very best gold-headed walking-stick.

Then she set it off. But, as it started, the crook of the walking-stick caught in the elastic of her trousers and carried her up into the sky with it.

'Oh dear, oh dear!' cried the people, 'what an unhappy accident! What will become of her?'

'It's all right,' said the neighbour who had given her the rocket; 'I did it all on purpose. It is a magic rocket; in fact, it is the only thing which knows where she lives, and it will carry her home.'

Which is just what happened. The rocket soared

through the dark sky with her and then landed plump in the rain-water tank on her step-parents' roof.

And there they found her and took her out, and washed her, and fed her generally on tapioca pudding and cold mutton, and didn't talk to her, and combed her hair *much* too often.

The Glass-Ball Country

I**N** a country where I was once walking there was an enormous castle on the top of a rock. It was all ruined; but it was very difficult to climb the rock, and there was still enough of the walls left to make it quite hard to get in. And inside the walls an old charcoal burner had built himself a cottage, to live there with his wife and his little girl.

At the time he built it there were a tremendous lot of wars. Not just one big war, like we have nowadays sometimes, but any number of little ones going on at the same time and in the same country, so that sometimes you would find as many as three separate battles going on in the same field, and armies falling over each other to get at their own enemy.

The old charcoal burner did not like this, so he thought if he built his cottage up inside the ruined castle, the armies wouldn't find him and he would be out of the way of all these wars. So he built it, and was very careful not to tell anyone where he lived, in case they went and told one of the armies.

But one night late as he was coming back from the town, he met an old pedlar on the high road. The pedlar was very old and wobbly on the pins, and he asked the charcoal burner how far it was to the town.

'Ten miles,' said the charcoal burner.

The old pedlar groaned. 'Dearie me,' he said, 'I don't feel as if I could walk another step.'

Now the charcoal burner was in a great difficulty. If he left the old pedlar, he might die before ever he got to the town; but if he took him to his cottage, he might be a spy, who would tell an army where he lived.

But all the same, he thought it would be kinder to take the old man home and risk it.

So he took him up to his cottage and gave him supper; and then the old pedlar, who was very tired, went to bed.

No sooner was he in bed, however, than the charcoal burner's wife began to row him. 'You silly idiot!' she said. 'I'm sure he isn't a real pedlar at all, but a spy who will tell the armies where we are, and we shall all be killed!'

'Well, let's go and look at him,' said the husband.

So they went up to the pedlar's room and looked at him; and sure enough he had taken off his white beard and hung it at the end of his bed, and was really quite a young man.

'What are we going to do now?' said the charcoal burner.

'We must kill him!' said his wife. 'You go and get your axe, and cut him in half while he is asleep.'

So the old charcoal burner went and got his axe and came back, but when he saw the stranger lying asleep he found it very difficult to make up his mind to do it.

'My axe wants sharpening,' he said.

'Then sharpen it,' said his wife.

So he went down to the grindstone and sharpened and sharpened it till it was sharp as a razor. Then he came back.

'Now do it,' said his wife.

'I can't,' he said. 'You do it.'

So the charcoal burner's wife took the axe, but before she could do anything the stranger woke up, and they only just had time to get out of the room before he should see them.

'Never mind,' said the old woman, 'I will do it as soon as he is asleep again.' But, instead, while she was waiting she fell asleep herself, and didn't wake up till the morning, when the pedlar had already got up and put on his beard and was ready to start on his journey.

But before he went he took a big glass ball, bigger than a football, out of his pack.

'That is a present for your little girl,' he said: 'Thank you for being so kind to me'; and away he went.

'Oh dear, oh dear,' said the old charcoal burner to his wife, 'now he will tell the armies, and they will come and kill us all!'

But the little girl took the glass ball and put it on the mantelpiece, and loved it dearly. And as a matter of fact the stranger was not a spy at all, so it was very lucky they hadn't killed him. But it *did* happen that a few days later one of the armies fighting about the place saw the old castle, and so they said, 'Let's go up there and have a rest, where the enemy won't find us.'

So a whole lot of soldiers began to climb the rock.

'Here they come!' said the old woman. 'Now we shall all be killed. Oh, where can we possibly hide?'

'Haven't you seen there is a whole country inside the glass ball?' said the little girl. 'It's ever so tiny, only about an inch across: but we might hide there.'

'Good idea,' said her father: so they all three made themselves absolutely tiny and got into the country inside the glass ball. They made themselves so tiny they were just the right size for the country.

Meanwhile the soldiers reached the cottage, and they ate all the food, and put their muddy feet on the beds, and laughed and drank and behaved perfectly horribly. At last one of them said, 'Look at that glass ball: what fun it would be to throw it from the top of the rock, and watch it smash to little bits in the valley below!'

So he took the ball, with the country inside it, and the three people inside the country, and went to the edge of the rock and threw it over. And it fell down, down, down into the valley beneath, where it hit a big stone and was smashed to atoms!

But when the ball was smashed the country that was inside fell out and lay on the ground. It was about as big as a small frog, and first it was hidden under a leaf. But then it began to grow. That was a curious thing; by the afternoon it was quite three feet across. Of course the people grew with it, so they didn't notice what was happening, except that the leaf that at first covered the whole world had now shrunk until it only covered two fields. And all that night the country grew, till by morning it filled all the meadow where it was lying.

Just then a wounded soldier came hobbling along, with another soldier after him trying to kill him.

'Come in here,' called the little girl. So the wounded soldier got into the country, but when the one who was chasing him tried to get in he couldn't do it. And lo and behold, who should the wounded soldier be but the very stranger who had given the little girl the glass ball.

'What country is this?' she asked him.

'It's the Peace Country,' he said; 'no one can fight inside here.'

No more they could. Some of the farmers who were trying to get out of the way of the wars came in, but the armies couldn't.

And still the country went on growing, till now it covered the whole county, and the armies found themselves getting rather cramped for space to fight in. But still they went on fighting and still the country went on growing, till at last there was no room for them at all, and they were all pushed into the sea and the whole lot were drowned. But the Peace Country grew till it covered all the old warry country, and there the farmers and other quiet people all lived together happily, and they made the charcoal burner and his wife king and queen and the little girl princess.

'Now I am a princess,' she said, 'I think I will marry the stranger who gave me the lovely ball.'

But he had disappeared for good.

Nothing

WHEN the maid came in to do the dining-room in the morning, 'Good gracious!' she said, 'what a mess those children do leave the table in, to be sure!'

'What have they left on the table?' called the cook from the kitchen.

'Well, there's a drop of milk,' said the maid.

'*That's* not much to make a fuss about,' said the cook.

'There's also a dead Chinaman,' said the maid.

'Never mind,' said the cook; 'it might be worse. Has he just died, or was he always dead?'

'I think,' said the maid, 'he was born dead, and was

42

dead when he was a little boy, and finally grew up dead.'

'What else is there?' asked the cook.

'There's a tooth, and I think it has dropped out of some passing shark.'

'Dear, dear,' said the cook, 'children are *that* rampageous!'

'There is also,' said the maid, pulling up the blind and looking at the table more carefully, 'unless I am much mistaken, a live Chinaman.'

'Tut-tut!' said the cook; 'what a fuss you do make! And was *he* always alive?'

'I don't know,' said the maid. 'And there's a Stocking Left Over From Before.'

'Dearie me!' said the cook. 'What else?'

'Nothing,' said the maid.

'Well,' said the cook, 'don't you touch Nothing.'

So the maid didn't touch Nothing: she cleared away the drop of milk, and the dead Chinaman, and the shark's tooth, and the live Chinaman, and the Stocking Left Over From Before, but Nothing she left in the middle of the table, and laid the breakfast round it.

Just then the seven children came down to breakfast.

'Why, what *is* that in the middle of the table?' said the youngest, and wanted to play with it.

'That's Nothing,' said the eldest. 'Leave it alone.'

Then the father and mother came down to breakfast too.

'What is there for breakfast?' said the father.

'Amongst other things,' said the mother, 'there's Nothing. Would you like some?'

'No, thank you,' said the father, 'I prefer bacon.'

So he had some bacon, and she had some bacon, and the children ate their eggs.

When breakfast was over, the mother sent for the cook.

'How often have I told you,' she said, 'to throw Nothing away?'

So the cook obediently went up to the table, and picked up Nothing and threw it out of the window.

But she never breathed a word to her mistress about the drop of milk, and the dead Chinaman, and the shark's tooth, and the live Chinaman, and the Stocking Left Over From Before; she hid them under her apron, and when the father and mother were gone she gave them back to the seven children, for she was a nice cook.

'Oh, thank you,' sang the seven children; 'what a nice cook you are!'

So she kissed them all, and then went back to the kitchen.

The Hasty Cook

ONCE there was a little boy who was rather naughty. One night when he couldn't go to sleep, although he had hardly been in bed half an hour, he got up and said to himself:

'I'll creep down quietly to the kitchen so that nobody hears and cook myself some breakfast!'

So he pulled on a pair of trousers over his pyjamas and crept down to the kitchen; and although it was nearly grown-up dinner time, Cook had gone round the corner to see a friend, so there was no one there.

'I'll see what there is in the larder,' he thought, and went to look. There was nothing but a big bowl of lumps of sugar and a poor dead sparrow. So he went into the scullery to see what pots and pans there were, and when he got there all he found was one big saucepan standing on a shelf.

'That'll do, I think,' he said; and no sooner had he said it than the saucepan jumped off the shelf and came bumping after him into the kitchen.

'Hallo, what are *you* doing?' said the little boy.

'Well, you want me, don't you?' asked the saucepan.

'Yes,' said the little boy, 'get on the fire.'

'If I get on the fire empty,' said the saucepan, 'I shall burn a hole in myself. Won't you put something in me?'

'All right,' said the little boy; and going to the larder he fetched the dead sparrow and the lumps of sugar and put them into the saucepan. Then the saucepan hopped up on to the fire, and soon he could hear bubbly noises coming from its inside.

'Good!' said the little boy; and just at that moment the only button which held his braces on to his trousers burst and shot across the room, and he had to try and find it.

Now what really happened was that instead of finding his own button, he found another one, and the other one was magic, though, of course, he didn't know that. He didn't know how to sew, so what he did was this. He got a piece of fine string and threaded the button on it, then he gathered up the back of his trousers in a bunch in his hand and tied the string round the bunch. Then he buttoned on his braces and went on with his cooking.

'Shall I stir you?' he said to the saucepan.

'No, please,' said the saucepan in a muffled voice. 'I am getting on very nicely, thank you.'

Now a funny thing had begun to happen. The new button on the back of his trousers had begun to grow, and when he felt it with his fingers it was as large as a saucer.

'That's funny,' he thought. 'I didn't remember it was as large as that.'

But still it went on growing, and soon it was so large that one rim touched the floor behind his feet, and the other reached up to the top of his head.

Just then he heard the cook come running in, for the grown-ups were ringing for their dinner. Then he was frightened and tried to run away, but the button was so big and heavy he couldn't; and he only tumbled on his back *on* the enormous button *on* the kitchen table, unable to move; and Cook rushed in.

'Well, they *are* in a hurry!' said Cook, as she heard the bell ringing, and without looking what she was doing she slapped a dishcover over the little boy and carried him up on his button and set him on the table. Then, still not looking what she was doing, she tipped what was in the saucepan into another dish and carried that up too.

When the father took the cover off and just saw his little boy lying on an enormous button instead of his dinner he was so surprised he didn't know what to do. But they soon saw the button was still growing; by now it nearly covered the table.

'Quick!' said the mother, 'there's no time to lose!' And seizing the carving knife she cut the string and set the little boy free. Then she and the father seized the perfectly enormous button and managed with great difficulty to roll it out of the house, and start it rolling down the hill; and they never saw it again. Then she said, 'Let's see what's on the other dish'; so they looked inside and were astonished to find a beautiful birdcage made of sugar, with a sugar bird inside.

'How lovely!' they said. 'But it won't be much for us for dinner.' So they went out and had dinner that night at a restaurant, and they gave the sugar birdcage to the little boy and sent him off up to bed with it.

The Spider's Palace

ONCE upon a time there was a little girl who lived in a tangly forest all by herself; and the only thing she was afraid of was the snakes. So she built her nest right on the end of some thin twigs, so thin that the snakes couldn't get along them to bite her, and there she sat in her nest and did her sewing, or learnt lessons out of a book she had, and sometimes played little tunes on a mouth organ; while all the snakes in the forest used to come out along the branches as far as they dared and hiss at her angrily: but they couldn't get to her, and though she was afraid she didn't show it.

One particularly nice and sunny day she was sitting like this, doing something or other, when all of a sudden she had a visitor. He was a big brown spider, and he had let himself down on his rope out of the sky; or so it seemed, for she couldn't see where the rope went to. But he held the end with all his legs and spoke to her kindly.

'Would you like,' he said, 'to leave this little nest where there are so many snakes about, and come and live in my palace with me?'

'I should be delighted,' said the little girl. 'But how can I get there?'

'Easily,' he said. 'Catch hold of me and I will pull you up.'

So she caught hold of him, and he began to roll up the rope with his legs, and soon they were swinging high up in the air, while all the snakes went to the tops of the trees and waved their heads at them and hissed ten times more angrily now that she was escaping from them altogether.

But still the spider went on winding in his rope, and higher into the air they went, and still higher.

At last, 'Here we are!' he said, and they found themselves on the doorstep of his palace.

The little girl was very much surprised; for truly the palace was a wonderful one. Apart from the fact of its size (and it was one of the biggest there ever have been), and the fact that it was up in the air (its lowest floor being ever so much above the highest mountains), there was one even more extraordinary thing about it: it was absolutely transparent—that is to say, you could see through it in all directions, clearer than through the clearest glass. So that if you were up in the attics you only had to move the rug on the floor and you could see what was happening in the dining-room at least ten floors below. Now the little girl thought, 'This will be great fun'; and so it was, especially when she went to bed at night: for, though the spider shut the door and put out the light, instead of having nothing to do except go to sleep, she could always lean out of bed and look down, down, down, to where the spider sat alone at the head of a large and grand table, eating a grand late dinner by himself: and when he had finished that he used to walk into the library and smoke a cigar, and it looked ever so funny to see the cigar smoke rise and then flatten out against a ceiling you could see through as plainly as if it wasn't there. In fact, she hardly ever went to sleep at all till every light in the house was put out; and even then there was generally some light on the earth beneath she could look at, or she could lie on her back and stare through the ceiling at the stars and moon.

But there was one room in the middle of the palace she couldn't see into; and this was why. It was covered with curtains. There were curtains over the walls and curtains that drew across the ceiling; and there was even a curtain which drew across the floor, in case anyone went into the cellars and tried to look up. She had often been into the room, and it looked just like any other room: but all the same she knew it was *very* mysterious, because once a week, after dinner in the evening, the spider used to go and lock himself in there and draw the curtains, and stay a whole hour: and what he did the little girl could never find out, although she was the most inquisitive little girl in all the world.

But, all the same, the spider was so kind to her and she was so fond of him she didn't like to worry him by asking too many questions. He let her do whatever she liked, and when she was tired of playing indoors she would run out on to the clouds and play on them. They were rather like hay to play in. Sometimes she used to bury herself while the spider ran about looking for her; but what was even better fun was to climb up a steep cloud and then roll off,

she would run out
on to the clouds

head over heels, into the cloud below. But when little bits
of cloud got down her neck they tickled like mad.

On fine days, of course, when there were no clouds she
had to stay indoors—just the opposite of what *we* do on
the ground. And sometimes the clouds were too thin, and
then she couldn't go out either, in case she fell through;
and sometimes they raced by so fast, that if once she had

got on them she would never have been able to get back.
So she often had to stay in, and then she used to sit and
plot to herself how to find out what the spider did once
a week in that secret room; though all the same she
didn't really want to do anything that would make him
angry.

At last she had an idea. When it came to the night for
him to go there, she crept quietly out of bed and downstairs. It was very, very difficult, with walls you could see
through. If he had looked up from his dinner any moment
he might have seen her. But somehow she managed it, and
got into the secret room and hid under the sofa: and she
had hardly been there a few minutes when she heard him
coming. So she flattened herself on the ground and hardly
dared breathe.

He walked into the room and she managed to peep out
and look at him; and what was her astonishment to see he
was no longer a spider at all, but a man! He looked the
same sort of man as he had looked a spider: and when she
watched him she wondered she could have ever really
believed he was born a spider at all, and wasn't a man
turned into one; and on the whole she was sorry.

He stayed a man for a whole hour, and then he turned
back into a spider and went to bed; and the little girl
crept out and went to bed, too.

But, while she was lying awake thinking about it, a
queer thing happened. All the clear walls and ceilings of
the palace started to go milky: and when she woke up in
the morning she couldn't see through them at all. They
had all turned into white marble. She got up and went to
look for the spider, and, as you might expect, he was now
changed back into a man altogether. He didn't say anything, and she didn't either, even when they found the
palace had sunk down and was now in the middle of a

valley. They neither mentioned the change, and she went on living in the palace just the same. It was a very nice palace as palaces go; but, after all, marble palaces on the ground are much commoner than ones up in the sky that you can see through: and, as I said before, on the whole she was sorry.

The Ants

I N a little farm near a big wood there lives a farmer
with his two sons. He is a very fat old man, and what
he likes best to do is to sit by the fire in the evening,
dozing. But what his sons like best is to go out into the
wood at night poaching. One of the sons is called Harry,
and the other is called Will.

One night, Harry came back from poaching alone, and
rather late.

'Where is Will, Father?' he asked. 'Hasn't he come in?'

'No,' said the old fat farmer. 'Wasn't he with you?'

'Yes,' said Harry, 'but I lost him.'

They both went to bed; but next morning Will had
not come back, nor all that day, and they were rather
worried.

That evening Harry went off to the wood as usual; and

though the poor old farmer sat up half the night, this time Harry did not come back either.

So the next night the old farmer thought, 'I must go out and look for those two boys myself.' And he set out for the wood. Now the boys were clever poachers, and knew how to move about the wood at night without being heard: but the farmer didn't, and made such a scrunching and a crackling, treading on dead sticks and pushing through the bushes, that almost at once a gamekeeper pounced out on him.

'What are you doing here?' he asked.

'I'm looking for my two sons,' said the old farmer: 'they used to come to poach in this wood. Have you caught them, by any chance?'

'No,' said the gamekeeper, 'I haven't caught anyone for ever so long.'

'Then, will you help me look for them?' asked the farmer.

'Certainly,' said the keeper, and they started off together to look for Harry and Will.

Presently they came to a little sandy hill in the middle of the wood, with four pine trees on top. They stood there and looked out across miles and miles of tree tops; but they could see no signs of the two lost brothers.

Beyond the hill was a little dell, which was rather steep and difficult to climb into.

'I will go and look in the dell,' said the keeper. 'You wait here. I won't be more than five minutes.'

So the farmer waited five minutes, and then he waited ten minutes, and still the keeper had not come back. When he had waited twenty minutes he said:

'Oh dear, I suppose I shall have to go into this dreadful dell myself.'

He started to scramble, but almost at once he slipped

and rolled right down to the bottom. He was not hurt, but he was very frightened, expecting something awful to happen.

At first nothing seemed to happen at all; but then he noticed that everything was getting bigger. The trees seemed to shoot right up into the sky, and to be getting as thick round as towers; the grass grew up to his knees, and then up to his eyes, and soon was towering over his head like a forest itself. A huge pine needle lay in his way, and he bruised his knee badly against it. Of course, what really happened was that he was getting smaller; in fact, before very long he was not quite so tall as one of the little hairs on the back of your hand.

He crept under the wing of a dead daddy-long-legs, wondering what would happen.

All of a sudden an ant came by, and as soon as it saw him it picked him up with its great jaws by the seat of his trousers and rushed away with him. You know the way ants run, not going round things but climbing over the highest thing in their way—so this ant ran now, swinging the poor farmer from side to side and bumping him badly. At last the ant reached his heap, and rushed in, dragging the poor old man along one of the little sandy tunnels. The grains of sand seemed as large to him as big rocks, and scratched and bruised him horribly.

Then they came out into a huge kind of hall. It was very dark, but he could just see rows and rows of ants' eggs, looking like people in white sacks, or beds in a hospital. At the far end sat the Queen; and it was to her the ant carried the old farmer, rushing along at a tremendous pace.

'No time! No time!' sang out the Queen, busily twiddling all her legs at once. 'No time to eat him now: lock him up with the others.'

So the soldier-ant carried him off down another passage, and into a dark little room, and put a heavy blade of grass across the door to stop him getting out. In this room there were also Harry and Will and the gamekeeper, and they all were very sad at thinking how horrid it would be when the Queen *had* got time to eat them, and how sharp and strong her great jaws were.

But the old farmer was full of ideas.

'First,' he said, 'all stand in a row, and then let us each put our head under the coat of the one in front of us, so that we look like one big caterpillar.'

So they did this, and a very fierce caterpillar they looked.

'Now, let us break down the blade of grass,' said the old man. So they all ran at it together, and at last managed to break it down and get out into the passage. Then they began charging down the passage, singing 'God Save the King' at the tops of their voices: and when the ants saw this extraordinary-looking animal coming they fell over each other in wonder and terror, and didn't try to stop them. So they charged along till they came to the great hall, and galumphed through it, knocking over the nurse-ants and banging into the eggs, still singing 'God Save the King'.

'Bite him in half! Bite him in half!' screamed the Queen; and several soldier-ants rushed up to do so. But all the men did was to separate when the ants bit, and then join up again as soon as they could.

'It's no good!' cried the soldier-ants; 'as soon as you bite him in half he joins up again.'

'Oh, *does* he, indeed!' cried the Queen, very angry. 'Then I'll see if *you* can, too.'

She rushed off her throne in a great rage, and began biting the poor soldiers in half with her own jaws. But while she was doing that the farmer and his two sons and the keeper made their way out of the hall by the passage they had been dragged in by.

But alas! They couldn't find their way out of the heap. There were passages running in all directions, and twists and corners everywhere, and soon they were hopelessly lost.

'Oh dear, oh dear!' cried the keeper in despair. 'Now they will get us'—for they could hear an angry murmur as the whole ant army came after them down the passages.

Then—and why it happened no one could tell, but it was really very lucky—they began to swell again. They were soon too tall for the passage they were in, and burst through the ceiling into the room above. And they went on growing, faster and faster, till soon they burst the top off the anthill, and scattered it in all directions. Before long there they were, standing, back at their ordinary heights again, while the poor ants rushed round their feet in the ruins of their palace, trying to save the Queen and the babies in the white sacks.

'Let's go home quickly,' said the farmer, 'before it happens again.'

'Good night!' said the keeper.

'Good night!' said the two poachers and the farmer, and went home.

After that, of course, no one ever went near that dangerous dell again: and though they have gone poaching every night from then till now, nothing has ever happened to the two boys in the other part of the wood, and the old farmer, who is now fatter than any other farmer in the country, is able to sit quietly at home in the evenings, just as he wants, dozing by the fire. If you saw him you would *never* believe he had once been so small that an ant had carried him off by the seat of his trousers.

the Invitation

THERE was once a little girl who slept in a very large room all alone. Sometimes she woke up in the night, and then she would feel very dull at having nothing to do except go to sleep again. So one night when she woke up, she sat up in bed and looked at the moonlight coming in at the window. While she was doing that there was a sudden *Pop!* and the top button of her pyjamas flew off. But, instead of falling on the bed, it floated gently across the room and out of the window; and once it was out of the window, there it stuck in the air, almost within reach. So the little girl got out of bed and went to the window to try and get it back. But, try as she would, she just couldn't reach it. So she climbed on to the window-sill to try and reach farther, and in doing that she tumbled right out.

59

Don't *you* try it!

When she had floated slowly down to the ground she looked about her, but the button was nowhere to be seen. Only the moonlight shone through the trees of the drive, and the wind rustled gently their leaves. For a minute she stood wondering what to do; and then she heard steps coming up the drive, so she hid behind a tree to see who it was. What was her surprise when the steps passed her, and she couldn't see anything at all! Only a postman's cap that floated along about the height of a man's head.

'Well,' she thought, very sensibly, 'I suppose this postman is invisible, and has an invisible uniform, but he has taken another postman's cap by mistake.'

So she stepped out into the moonlight, where he could see her, and asked if he had any letters for her.

'Yes,' he said, 'here is one'; and putting into her hand an invisible letter he walked away down the drive.

Of course the trouble with an invisible letter is that you can't read it, so the little girl was rather worried what to do. At last she decided she would go and see her very best friend, who was one of the gateposts down at the end of the drive. So, holding the letter very tight (because if she dropped it she would never be able to find it again), she walked down the drive after the postman, and climbed on to her friend.

'Dear gatepost,' she said, 'do help me to read this letter.'

And immediately the letter became visible, and she read it.

'*Dear little girl*,' it said, '*we are giving a party in our castle tonight. Will you come?*'

That was all: it didn't say who it was from, or where the castle was, or anything. Now the little girl knew the country round well, and there wasn't any castle there anywhere. That is to say, at any rate there were none on the ground; there might be some in the air—that she didn't know. So she climbed a tall tree to have a look.

At the top of the tree there was a railway-station, with a train just going to start: so she got in, and away the train went across the sky till it came to another station, and there she got out.

'Can you please tell me the way to the castle?' she said to the stationmaster.

'Which castle?' he asked. 'There are nine near this station.'

So she showed him the letter. He scratched his head.

'Well,' he said, 'that's the queerest letter I ever have seen, so I expect it comes from the queerest castle. And *that* one is only just round the corner.'

So he told her the way to go, and she soon came to it.

It was indeed the queerest of all castles, for it was upside down.

The gate was at the top, with big towers below it, and a flag at the bottom.

'Well,' she thought, 'I suppose the best way to get in is to turn upside down too.'

So she did, and soon found herself walking in at the gate quite comfortably.

The party that was going on in the big hall inside was a simply lovely one. Each person was dressed all in one colour, and these colours were of the brightest. There would be one person in bright lilac, and another in blue, and another in peacock, and another in green, and another in yellow, and another in orange, and another in scarlet, and another in crimson. They all nodded to the little girl and told her they were glad she had come. The ones who were talking walked about the floor, but if they wanted to dance they did it on the ceiling, where there was more room, and if they wanted something to eat they walked up the walls to little tables which stuck out here and there.

Presently the little girl found a nice man to dance with, so they went up to the ceiling and danced round and round the electric light. Then they walked down the wall to one of the little tables and there ate ices.

'What will you do,' he asked presently, 'when the Special Licence gives way?'

'What is the Special Licence?' asked the little girl.

'It's a sort of spell,' he said, 'giving leave for the castle to be upside down. And it gives way at one o'clock—why, it's nearly one o'clock now!'

'Oh, I'll wait and see what happens,' said the little girl very sensibly, and began hurriedly to eat another ice before the time should be up.

When it struck one, the first thing that happened was that all the people shrank and shrank and turned into mice; but they still stayed their lovely colours, and chased each other round and round the little girl, looking very pretty. Next the castle got smaller and smaller, and finally came to bits till there was nothing left but a single bit of broken china; and the mice all ran away.

'Thank you very much,' she called after them: 'I *did* enjoy myself.'

Then the little girl found she was at home, and sitting under the kitchen table.

So she stole quietly up to bed again, and luckily no one heard her.

The Three Innkeepers

There was once a farmer who got tired of farming, so he thought he would go to the town and start an inn.

But when he got there, he found that there were two inns there already: and one of them was called *The King's Head*, and one was called *The King's Arms*.

'Very well,' he said, 'I shall call *my* inn *The King's Legs*.'

So he had a beautiful sign painted with the King's legs on it, and hung up outside.

Now this turned out very well. Nobody had ever heard of an inn being called *The King's Legs* before, so all strangers used to come in out of curiosity, to ask why on earth the inn had got such a strange name. Then, of course, they had at least to buy a drink, and sometimes they stayed the night so as to be able to use notepaper with such a lovely address when writing to their friends: and so *The King's Legs* inn became the most prosperous in the town, and the new innkeeper got rich and the old innkeepers began to get poor.

So they put their heads together, and wondered what was the reason. 'I know,' said the landlord of *The King's Arms*. 'It is because he has got such a funny name for his inn. I'm going to change the name of mine.'

So he decided to call his inn in future *The King's Stomach*; and he took down the old sign to get a new picture painted. 'Mind you make it a big one,' he said to the sign painter, 'or else it won't look royal'—though, as a matter of fact, the king of that country was not particularly fat at all.

Then he hung up the new sign and waited to see what happened.

But what happened was not at all what he expected. Some courtiers of the King happened to be travelling that way; and, when they saw the sign, they were very angry and shocked. 'What!' they cried: 'The impudent creature! Fancy calling *that* great fat stomach the King's! As if everyone didn't know he had the slimmest and most elegant little stomach in the kingdom!'

'What shall we do?' asked one of the courtiers. 'Shall we arrest him for high treason and have his head cut off?'

'We might do that,' said another of the courtiers. 'But, on the whole, wouldn't it be more fun just to throw some stones through his windows?'

The others all agreed; so they got off their horses and began throwing stones through the windows of *The King's*

Stomach inn until there wasn't a single pane of glass left unbroken. Then they rode on.

So the landlord said to the landlord of *The King's Head*: 'Well, *my* plan didn't work very well. Have *you* got one?'

'Yes, I have,' said the landlord of *The King's Head*. 'I have thought of a very funny idea.' He went and bought a curious sort of gilt bird, and shut it up tight in a glass case, and put a label on it, 'Weathercock', and put it in the window of his inn.

Now it wasn't long before some people came by. 'Hullo,' they said, 'that's a funny thing to do, to keep your weathercock shut up in a glass case where the wind can't get at it! I wonder why he does that?'

So they went in to ask.

'Why do you call that funny gold bird in a glass case a "weathercock"?' they asked, when they had ordered some beer.

'Because,' said the landlord, 'just what it is, *whether cock* or hen, I can't decide.'

Lots of people came in to ask the same question, and he gave them all the same answer.

So now the landlord of the new inn, *The King's Legs*, found all the people going back to *The King's Head*, and himself not getting rich any more.

So he got a large gilt egg, and went along quietly at night, and slipped it in the glass case along with the bird.

Next day some people came by and asked the usual question and were given the usual answer.

'But, you silly old ass!' they cried out to the innkeeper, 'anyone can see it's a hen! Why, it's laid an egg!'

And they were so angry they took up several of the big glass beer tankards that were about and started hitting the landlord with them on the head. It didn't hurt his head much because it was very hard, but it broke all the tankards, and he went along to see his friend about it all.

'It's a funny thing,' said his friend, 'but whatever we do it always seems to end in glass being broken.'

'That means,' said the other one, 'there must be some sort of magic in it all.'

'Well, in that case,' said the first one, 'we had better go and see the Village Witch, and ask for her advice.'

So they went to the Village Witch, who happened to be also the District Nurse.

'There is only one thing to be done,' said the witch. 'We must kill him.'

'Well, will you do it for us if we pay you?' asked the innkeepers.

'Certainly,' said the witch, and putting on her nurse's uniform she bicycled round to *The King's Legs*. There she found the landlord in the parlour at the back.

'Dear, dear!' she said. 'I am sorry to hear you are so ill.'

'Am I?' said the landlord: '*I* hadn't heard.'

'Perhaps not, but *I* had!' said the witch firmly: 'You had better go to bed.'

So he went to bed, and she nursed him a bit and then said she would come back the next morning to see how he was.

The next day she came in the morning and went up to his room, looking very sad.

'You can't think,' she said, 'how sorry I was when I heard you had died in the night.'

At that the innkeeper looked very pale and frightened.

'What!' he said. 'Died in the night! Are you sure? Nobody told me.'

'No,' she said firmly; 'but they told *me*! I'll send the

undertaker round this afternoon to measure you for your coffin.'

As it happened the undertaker was busy that afternoon and couldn't come: but he came the next morning.

'Good morning,' he said, 'I have come to bury you.'

'What!' cried the innkeeper, who was just as clever as the witch; 'hadn't you heard?'

'Heard what?' said the undertaker.

'Why, I was buried yesterday afternoon! When you didn't come, I got the undertaker from the next town, and *he* buried me.'

The undertaker was very sorry at that because he didn't like losing a job, but there was nothing to be done if the innkeeper had been buried already: so he just went away.

Then the innkeeper got up and dressed and went down and started serving drinks in the bar. Presently the witch and the two other innkeepers looked in, to see if he was safely buried yet.

When they saw him quite well and serving drinks they were very upset.

'Good gracious!' exclaimed the witch, 'what are *you* doing here?'

'What!' exclaimed the innkeeper. 'But surely you must have heard! I am the new landlord of *The King's Legs!* They buried the last one yesterday afternoon, poor chap!'

At that the two other innkeepers and the witch were so upset that, without saying a word, they all three ran hand in hand down the village street to the village pond and drowned themselves there: and the landlord of *The King's Legs* got a small paintbrush and wrote on the bottom of his sign in white paint:

Under Entirely New Management

67

Inhaling

ONCE there were two children out for a walk by themselves, when they saw an enormous policeman. He was at least six times as big as any other policeman in the world.

'I know what's happened,' said the girl. 'He's been inhaling too much!'

'What's inhaling?' said the boy.

'You know,' said the girl, 'when we have a cold, and they pour some funny-smelling stuff into a jug of hot water, and make us breathe over it. That's inhaling.'

'Quite right, miss,' said the policeman, in a six-times-big voice, 'I have been inhaling too much: *much* too much!

Would you like some of the stuff?' And he gave them a small glass pot.

'Thank you,' she said. 'We're rather small, you see: there'd be no harm in trying a little.'

So they went home.

That night, when they were both in the bath, they poured some of the stuff into the hot water of the bath and immediately began to sniff it.

'This is fine!' said the little boy: '*Aren't* we growing nicely?'

And so they were; they were soon as tall as grown-up people. But the only trouble was that Nurse, who was giving them their baths, was swelling too; and as she was big to begin with she was now enormous.

'Put your head out of the window!' cried the boy. So the nurse did, and then, of course, she stopped smelling the stuff and stopped growing.

But the children didn't. They stood in the bath and got taller and taller.

'This ceiling *does* hurt my head,' said the girl.

And no wonder, for they were pressed hard up against it.

All of a sudden *crack!* went the ceiling, and pop! came their heads up into the room above! This room was their father's study, and there he sat working.

'Bless me, children!' he said, when he saw their heads coming up through the floor. 'What will you do next?'

'I don't know, Father,' said the girl, whose face was now above the top of his writing table.

'Bless me!' he said again. 'What a funny smell!'—for the smell of the stuff began to come up through the hole in the floor.

On that, of course, he began to swell too.

'Bless me!' he said. 'Fancy starting to grow again, at my age!'

And indeed he was soon about twice his ordinary height.

Just then the boy's big toe got caught in the chain of the bath plug and pulled it up, and all the water ran away, and the magic stuff with it, and so no one grew any more.

But now they were in a great difficulty. The mother was still ordinary size, because she hadn't been there. And the nurse hadn't had time to grow very much before she put her head out of the window; but even then she was taller than the tallest soldier you ever saw. As for their father, he was twice the size he had been, and couldn't sit in his study at all comfortably, and could hardly crawl through the door. But as for the children, they were so big that, with their feet in the bath, the bathroom ceiling was only just up to their waists and their heads were just on the point of bumping the ceiling of the study above.

'What a funny family we are,' they said, 'with the children bigger than their father and mother!'

'However,' they said, 'we can't go on living in the same house, that's certain'; so they built a new house, and a very funny house it was. The nursery, of course, was enormous; it reached from the cellar right up to the roof, and the nursery table was almost as high as an ordinary room, and they had washbasins as plates. As for baths, they had to go and have cold ones in the pond; it would have taken *much* too much hot water to give them one in the house. Then came the study for their father, that was just about double size: there was a double-size table, and a double-size chair, and double-size books, and double-size papers, and double-size pipes and matches and tobacco boxes, and double-size pictures and even a double-size wastepaper basket. But the poor little mother had just an ordinary-size drawing-room and bedroom, and had to be ever so careful, when she went into the nursery, that the children didn't tread on her.

But as for the swollen nurse, it was much less trouble to send her away and get a new one of the ordinary size, so that's what they did.

The China Spaniel

THERE was once a school that was rather cross and dull, and it was run by one old woman.

Now it so happened that one of the children at this school was a china spaniel, the kind that has a gold chain round its neck, and doesn't look as if it had much sense. As a matter of fact, this one had practically no sense at all: he was easily the stupidest pupil in the whole school, and could never learn his lessons properly.

One day they were all given some poetry to learn for homework; and the china spaniel really did try his hardest: but when he came into school the next day he couldn't remember a single line of it.

In fact, the only thing that came into his head to say was:

Pink and green silver-paper toffee-paper!
Pink and green silver-paper toffee-paper!
Pink and green ...

'What!' screamed the old woman: '*That* isn't what I gave you to learn!'

But there must have been some sort of magic in the words, for immediately all the other children in the school, the good ones and the clever ones and everybody, rose up from the desks, and all began chanting together at the tops of their voices:

Pink and green silver-paper toffee-paper!
Pink and green silver-paper toffee-paper!

—and out into the street they all rushed, dancing and singing at the tops of their voices.

'What's this? What's this?' said a policeman. 'What's all the row about?'

'Pink and green silver-paper toffee-paper!' shouted the children.

And thereupon the policeman began to dance too, and chanted it with the children.

'What's this? What's this?' cried the Chief of Police, who happened to be passing: 'One of my policemen dancing? What does this mean, sir!'

'Pink and green silver-paper toffee-paper!' replied the policeman: and no sooner did he hear it than the Chief of Police started chanting it too, with all the rest, for by now there were quite a lot of other people of the town who had joined the procession and went along chanting

Pink and green silver-paper toffee-paper!

with the china spaniel, who had started it all, marching proudly at their head.

At last they came to the Royal Palace, whereupon the King came out on his balcony ready to make a speech.

'My loyal subjects, I see you gathered together before my palace in great numbers. Well, as you know, I am a kind king and always anxious to give you what you want, so what is it?'

'Pink and green silver-paper toffee-paper!' cried the people; 'pink and green silver-paper toffee-paper!'

'*What* did they say they wanted?' whispered the Prime Minister, who was a little deaf, at the King's elbow.

'Pink and green silver-paper toffee-paper?' asked the Prime Minister's secretary in polite surprise.

And then, in a twinkling, they were all dancing and chanting and shouting in the palace as well as outside it:

> *Pink and green silver-paper toffee-paper,*
> *Pink and green silver-paper toffee-paper,*
> *Pink and green silver-paper toffee-paper,*
> *Pink and green silver-paper toffee-paper,*
> *Pink and green silver-paper toffee-paper,*
> *Pink and green silver-paper toffee-paper!*

Nor was it long before the whole nation was singing it: and some enemies who were besieging the town at the time, hearing it, thought it must be some sort of national anthem, till they found themselves starting to sing it too; and, in short, it wasn't long before the whole world was singing it—the whole world, that is to say, except the old woman who kept the school.

'It would take more than the whole world going mad,' she said very firmly, 'to make *me* start dancing and playing the goat!'

And she went on trying to run her school just as before it happened, the silly old thing.

The Magic Glass

THERE is a little boy I know who always looks very carefully in wastepaper baskets, 'because, he says, 'you never know what valuable things you may find that some silly grown-up has thrown away.'

One day he found what looked like the glass off the end of an electric torch. 'That will make a most useful magnifying glass,' he said, and put it in his pocket.

That night he woke up; and not being able to get to sleep again he thought he would look at a few things through his glass. The first thing he looked at was a wooden rabbit lying on the end of his bed; but the strange thing was that, when he looked through the glass, instead of the toy, what he saw was a real live rabbit, sitting up on its hind legs and wobbling its nose at him!

Then he took the glass from his eye: and lo and behold, it was only a wooden one again.

'This *is* a funny glass,' thought the little boy.

Then he looked through it at a china duck there was on the mantelpiece: and, sure enough, there was a real duck, which would have jumped down on to the floor if he hadn't quickly taken the glass from his eye and turned it back to china again.

By this time the little boy was so excited with his glass that he got out of bed and crept down to the room where his father and mother were lying asleep. 'For,' he thought, 'if it turns toys into real, I wonder if it turns real people into toys?' And he put it to his eye and looked at his father and mother. And so it was: they were immediately wooden Mr. and Mrs. Noah out of the Ark. To make sure, he took a pin, and keeping the glass firmly in his eye he tried to stick it into his mother. But it wouldn't go in, for she was now quite hard: it only scratched a little paint off. Then he took the glass away, and they were his mother and father again. But just to make sure he stuck the pin in again. This time it went right in, and his mother sat up with the most awful yell.

'You naughty boy!' she said. 'What are you doing out of bed? And *what* did you stick a pin into me for?'

'I'm awfully sorry, Mother,' he said, 'but I thought you were Mrs. Noah! You were, a minute ago, you know!'

'Mrs. Noah?' said his mother. 'Stuff and nonsense! You must have been dreaming! Go back to bed at once.'

So he went back to bed, and soon was asleep. In the morning, when he went to school, he put the glass in his pocket.

Now, on the way to school there was a dog which the little boy simply *hated*. Every day when it saw him coming it used to poke its nose through the gate and growl and bark, and he never knew when it might jump out and bite him. So when he got near, and the dog began to bark, he looked at it through his glass, and all at once it turned into one of those funny china dogs you see sometimes on the mantelpiece in cottages. So the little boy picked it up, and threw it on the ground, and smashed it to bits. He wondered very much what would happen, now that it was smashed, when he took the glass away from his eye. What *did* happen was that it turned into a nice fur rug. So he hid it behind the fence. 'Good!' he thought: 'I'll pick it up on my way home and give it to Mother, to make up for jabbing her with that pin.'

When he got to school he forgot about the glass till halfway through lessons, when he took it out of his pocket and looked at the mistress through it. Immediately she turned into a golliwog.

The little boy was not very surprised, but you may imagine all the other children were! They made such a noise in their astonishment that the headmistress came into the room, and hearing her coming he slipped the glass back into his pocket.

'Now then, children!' she said, 'what's all this noise?' (It wasn't a very nice school.)

'The mistress has just turned into a golliwog!' shouted the children.

'Nonsense!' said the headmistress, who was a very cross old woman; but just then the little boy looked at the mistress again through his glass, and turned her again into a golliwog.

'Good gracious me! What's this?' said the headmistress, and went up to take hold of the golliwog: but when she got close, of course, the little boy could see her through the glass too, and immediately she turned into a Dismal Desmond.

At that, of course, the children were awfully pleased, and wanted to have them to play with: but the little boy said no, they mustn't go near or they'd all be turned into dolls, and all the other children said how clever the little boy was to have done it. So he kept on looking at them till lesson time was over; and then he went home, not forgetting to pick up the fur rug to give his mother.

That night, when he was in bed, his mother remembered his trousers wanted a button sewing on, so she came upstairs and fetched them, and then she found the glass in his pocket, and took it downstairs with her.

'What a funny glass!' she said, and put it to her eye, and looked at herself in the looking glass.

That was a most awful thing to happen: for not only did she turn into wooden Mrs. Noah immediately, but the glass simply became a painted glass in Mrs. Noah's eye. And so she would have to stay, because the wooden Mrs. Noah, of course, couldn't move, and as long as she didn't move she was staring at herself in the looking glass, and, as long as she stared at herself, Mrs. Noah she would stay.

As a matter of fact she was Mrs. Noah all night, and still Mrs. Noah when the maids came down in the morning to sweep the room.

'There's that naughty boy left one of his toys in the drawing-room,' they said, and went to move it: but as soon, of course, as they moved it away from the looking glass it turned back into a person.

'Good gracious!' they said. 'It's the mistress!'

And she rubbed her eyes, and said she felt very sleepy because she had sat up all night. Meanwhile the glass rolled away into a corner, and happened to stop just in the mouth of a mouse hole, and no one thought of it any more.

That afternoon the little boy's mother had a whole lot

of people coming to tea. They were very stiff and grand people that the little boy didn't like at all; but all the same he thought he would creep downstairs to the drawing-room door and have a look at them. So he did, and watched them from where he couldn't be seen. But the little boy wasn't the only inquisitive one. Just at the same moment the little mouse came up his hole, and thought he would have a look at them too: and across the hole was the magic glass, so he looked through that.

Immediately all the people turned into the funniest lot of dolls you have ever seen: dutch dolls and wax dolls and rag dolls, and even china ornaments. And that wasn't all. There were some pictures on the wall which the mouse could see, too: and while the real people turned into toys, the people in the pictures all stepped down into the room, in their funny old-fashioned dresses, and started to eat the tea. At that the little boy was so pleased that he laughed and clapped his hands, and the noise frightened the mouse, who ran away into the back of his hole, and so all was as before.

But presently the mouse came back and thought he would have another look. Just then the little boy's father came in from the office, and was standing in the drawing-room door when all the people turned into toys again, and the pictures started once more coming out of their frames. Meanwhile, the mouse was so excited he kept turning round to tell the other mice what he was seeing, and then looking back, and then turning round again, so that the boy's father was nearly astonished out of his wits, seeing them turn from people into toys and toys into people again as fast as the wink of an eye. But at last the mouse went away: and then they all stayed people, and when the tea party was over went home as if nothing had happened.

But the little boy's father was really rather frightened. 'There's something magic about this house,' he said to himself; and as soon as he could he found another house, and they all went to live in that and left the old one empty.

But no one noticed the magic glass sticking in the mouth of the mouse hole: and if someone else comes and lives in that house, and the mouse comes up his hole to have a look at them, I suppose the same thing will happen to them!

The Christmas Tree

I<small>T</small> was Christmas Eve, and the Christmas tree was all decorated ready for Christmas Day. But no sooner had everyone gone to bed than the toys hung on the tree began to talk to each other.

'What fun it would be,' they said, 'if we all got down and hid.'

So they all climbed down off the tree, leaving it quite bare, and went and hid—some behind cupboards, and some under the hot-water pipes, and some behind the books in the shelves in the library, and anywhere they could think of.

In the morning the children came down, wishing each other a Happy Christmas: but when they saw their lovely

81

tree all bare, without so much as a cracker left on it, they cried and cried and cried.

When they heard the children crying the toys all felt thoroughly ashamed of the naughty trick they had played: but all the same they didn't quite like to come out of their hiding places while anyone was about. So they waited till everyone had gone to church and then they slipped out.

'I know!' said the Noah's Ark, speaking in all his voices at once, 'I have an idea!'

So he led the other toys out of the house, and into the town, and there they separated and found their way into every toy shop and sweet shop there was, by the back door. Once inside, they invited all the toys and all the sweets to come to a grand party they were giving, and led them back to the house.

'Here is where we are giving the party,' they said, pointing to the Christmas tree. So all the new toys climbed up on to the boughs of the tree and hung there. Indeed, there was hardly room for them all, for now there were ten times as many as there had been before.

All through church the children went on crying quietly behind their prayer books, and came home feeling still very sad; but when they saw their Christmas tree with ten times as many presents on it as there had been before, and ten times as many candles, all kindly lighting each other, they laughed and clapped their hands and shouted with joy, and said they had never seen such a lovely Christmas tree in all their whole lives.

The Old Queen

BEYOND the farthest mountain that you can see there lies a country, which is perfectly flat, except for one mountain in the middle of it (which was not always there), and a small hill. On that small hill there is a palace, and in the palace there lives a queen. She is so old that no one can even remember when the King her husband died. She just goes on reigning and reigning. This is the story of why she never dies.

Once upon a time a very long while ago when the Queen was young, she was walking with the King her husband in the garden of the palace.

'Let me give you a present,' she said. So she picked an apple and gave it to the King.

'Now *I* must give *you* a present,' said the King, and

going to the chicken run he took out of it the only egg that was there.

'Here is my present,' he said to the Queen.

'That is a nice present,' said the Queen; 'I will keep it next my heart.'

So the Queen took the egg, and put it down the front of her dress to keep it warm. And at night she took it to bed with her; and in the morning when she put on her clothes she put it in the front of her dress again. And so at last the egg was hatched, but instead of a chicken the most marvellous bird came out of it; its feet were grey, and made of stone, and its feathers were green, and made of leaves, and its beak was shining, and see-through like water. So the Queen took it to show the King.

'That is the greatest wonder in my kingdom,' he said.

'It all comes of your giving me that egg,' said the Queen.

'And that came of your giving me the apple,' said the King.

'And that came of our walking in the garden,' said the Queen:

'So let's walk there again.'

So they went out into the garden, with the bird perched on the Queen's shoulder. When it felt the sunshine it began to sing, and its song was like all the rivers in the world falling off all the rocks in the world. To hear it made the King and Queen so happy they said:

'Let's go and ring the church bells.'

So they went to the church, and began to pull the bell ropes; but however hard they pulled, not a sound could they hear.

'That is funny,' said the King, and looked up to see what was wrong. And to his surprise he couldn't see the top of the steeple at all: it was stretching up high into the sky, right out of sight.

'They must be so far off by now that we can't hear them.'

'When I was a little girl,' said the Queen, 'my nurse told me that if I pulled a bell rope, and then when the bell began to ring I hung on, it would lift me up and up into the air. Let's try and see what happens.' So they each gave a good tug to their bell rope, and then instead of letting go they hung on, and the bell rope lifted them up into the air. But instead of going down again it carried them on, up and up, and all the while the wonderful bird flew round them singing its song, now round their heads and now round their feet, though they were three hours altogether going up.

First they could hear the bells faintly ringing in the distance.

'We are getting near them,' said the King.

Then as they got nearer the sound got louder and louder, till at last it was so loud they couldn't hear their lovely bird sing; and yet, when they were on the ground they couldn't hear the bells at all. Then they reached the bells themselves, and they climbed out on to the tip-top of the church steeple. They were so high up they couldn't see their country at all: it was all blue down below like the sky, and far down there were clouds floating under their feet.

The point of the steeple was sharp as a pin, but on top was a weathercock. So the King sat on the arm which said West, and the Queen sat on the arm which said East, and the bird on the arm which said South.

'I wish there was someone to sit on the arm which says North,' said the Queen: and no sooner had she said it than lo and behold there was a fairy sitting on it as if she had

'We are getting near them,' said the King.

been there all the time. And the fairy was green, and shiny and see-through like the bird's beak.

'Come and see my country,' said the fairy.

When she said that, one of the clouds which were far under their feet began to rise up, till soon it was close under them; and then they found that though it looked like cloud it was as solid to walk upon as ground. So they walked with the fairy till they came to her house; and the house was made of green cloud, and inside was a hearth, but the fire, instead of burning yellow or red, burnt a bright blue.

'Now,' said the fairy, 'I am going to make for each of you a magic robe, so that once you have worn it you will never die. But while I do it one of you must be blowing the fire.'

'*I* will,' said the Queen, and took the bellows. Now the curious thing about these bellows was that when you blew with them instead of air coming out it was water; and yet instead of putting the fire out it only made it burn the brighter.

'But someone must help me with these scissors,' said the fairy; 'they are far too large for me to manage alone.'

And so they were, for each blade was as long as a tall man.

'*I* will,' said the Queen. 'I understand scissors better than he does.'

'Then he must blow the fire,' said the fairy, 'I can only work while it is being blown.'

So the King took the bellows and began to blow the fire, but not looking what he was doing, watching the Queen and the fairy instead. Then the fairy took off a peg a piece of stuff so magic I mustn't describe it; and the Queen took hold of one handle of the scissors and the fairy the other and they made a robe for the Queen and she put it on.

'Now let's make one for the King,' said the fairy.

And they began to do it. But now, for the first time, the King began to look at what he was doing; and when he saw water pouring out of the bellows—'Good gracious!' he thought, 'that will put the fire out'—so he stopped blowing.

No sooner did he stop blowing than the cloud broke under them, and both he and the Queen began to fall.

'Don't be afraid!' said the bird, flying under them. 'You sit on my back.' So they did; and when they did, the bird changed into a mountain, the mountain that is there now; his feathers became trees, and his feet became rocks, and his beak became a waterfall.

As the King and Queen were walking down the side of the mountain she said to him: 'Now I will never die and you will: and that is the saddest thing that has ever happened to either of us.'

But every year they climbed the mountain, and planted flowers on the top in memory of their lovely bird. Forty years went by, and the King grew old, and the Queen grew old, and the King at last died: but the Queen didn't, she just went on getting older and older, and she is still alive now.

The School

ONCE there was a schoolmaster and a schoolmistress who hadn't any school.

'This is absurd,' they said. 'We *must* have a school': so they got a brass plate, and wrote the word 'SCHOOL' on it, and put it up on their gate.

The next day they rang a bell at nine o'clock in the morning for lessons to begin. But of course no one came. So for half the morning he taught her, and for the other half she taught him.

The next day he said, 'I am going out to see if I can't find someone to come to our school.' On the way he passed a toy shop, and in the window there was a fine big Noah's Ark; so he bought it and took it home. Then he

89

took out Mr. and Mrs. Noah, and Shem and Ham and Japhet, and all the animals, and put them in the desks in the schoolroom.

'Now,' he said, 'we have got a splendid big class to teach!'

So all that day they taught the things out of the Ark.

'I do think this is a well-behaved class,' said the schoolmistress. 'They sit ever so still and never make any noise at all!'

Which was perfectly true. They never made a sound. The only trouble was that when you asked them a question they still didn't make a sound, but just sat quiet and didn't answer.

'What do two and two make, Noah?' the schoolmistress asked.

But Mr. Noah said nothing.

'Next!' she said.

But Mrs. Noah said nothing either.

'Next! Next! Next!' said she. But Shem and Ham and Japhet and the two lions and the two elephants and the two mice and all the other animals said nothing either.

'What *I* think,' said the schoolmistress, 'is that we've got the stupidest class that ever was!'

So she popped them all back in the Ark and went out to look for something else.

Presently she came to a shop called 'Railway Umbrellas'. It was where they sell all the things people leave in railway carriages and never come back for: umbrellas, and handbags, and bananas, and babies, and concertinas, and parcels, and so on. So she went in. And sitting in the window she saw a dear little black kitten.

'Is that a railway kitten, too?' she asked the man.

'Yes, madam,' he said. 'Somebody left him in a basket on the rack of a train only the other day.'

'Well, I'll have that one then,' she said, and bought it and took it home. When lesson time came they took all the creatures out of the Ark and made the kitten sit in the middle of them.

'What do two and two make, Railway Kitten?' she asked.

'Meaow!' said the kitten.

'No, they don't, they make four!' she said. 'What is the capital of Italy?'

'Meaow!' said the kitten.

'Wrong! It's Rome. Who signed Magna Charta?'

'Meaow!' said the Railway Kitten.

'Wrong again,' she said, 'it was King John! I've never even heard of Mr. Meaow!' And she turned round and started to write a sum on the blackboard. But as soon as her back was turned the naughty Railway Kitten began to have a lovely game with all the wooden creatures out of the Ark. He knocked them down, and sent them skidding all over the floor: and when the schoolmistress looked round again he had climbed on his desk, dipped his tail in the inkpot, and now was swishing it about so as to flip ink all over the room.

'Oh, you *naughty* kitten!' she cried. 'If you're not good I'll send you back to your railway!' And she took him and shut him up in the kitchen.

Just then the front-door bell rang, and the schoolmaster went to see who it was. Outside there was a little girl, with a packet of school books under her arm.

'Please,' she said, 'I've forgotten the way to my school; may I come to yours instead?'

'Certainly! Certainly!' said the schoolmaster. So she came in, and hung her hat and coat on a peg, and changed her shoes, and went and sat down in the school-room.

Now, not only was she as good as the Ark creatures,

and sat perfectly still and quiet, but also when she was asked a question she answered it, and always got the answer right. And she never once let the Railway Kitten play during lessons, though out of lesson time of course she played with him a lot, and gave him his saucer of milk.

When the evening came she said: 'Is this a boarding school? Because if it is I don't think I shall bother to go home.'

'All right,' they said, and put her to bed.

Now, as I have told you, all day she had been good as good: but when she went to bed there was just one thing she was naughty about: she WOULD NOT get out of the bath when she was told. When she had been washed she just lay on her back and refused to move, and the poor schoolmistress simply *couldn't* make her. She lay there till the hot water turned her as pink as a lobster, and it wasn't till the water had got quite cold that she would come out. Then, of course, she was cold too, and shivered, and her teeth chattered when she got into bed.

The next day she was perfectly good again: but when night came the same thing happened—once she was in her bath she *would not* move.

'I am going to count one—two—three, and then pull up the plug!' said the schoolmistress. 'ONE! TWO!—'

And before she could say THREE the little girl jumped out in a terrible fright.

'That's a good plan,' thought the schoolmistress, 'I'll do it again.'

And so she did. Every night, when the little girl wouldn't get out, she counted ONE, TWO, and before she could say THREE out she jumped. And this went on for a whole week. But when it came to Saturday night, and she counted ONE! TWO! all the little girl said was 'SHAN'T!'

and lay so flat on the bottom of the bath that only her nose was above the water.

'THREE!' said the mistress, and pulled up the plug! Away the water rushed, down the waste pipe: and alas! away went the poor little girl with it. First her feet were sucked into the hole, and then her legs, and then her body, and in a moment she had disappeared altogether.

'OH, what *have* you done!' cried the schoolmaster. 'You have lost our only child!'

'I don't care!' said the schoolmistress in a stern voice. '*She should have got out of the bath when she was told!*'

The
Wonder-Dog

THERE was once a wonder-dog, who belonged to a little boy.

Every day when he came back from school, the little boy taught his dog the same lessons he'd learned himself that morning. When the little boy set him sums, the wonder-dog worked them out in his head and scratched the answers in the sand with his paw, and he always got them right. In fact he learned to do almost everything children can do except one: he *couldn't* learn to sing.

Now in that same village there was a proud cat who

had a very special tree which she wouldn't let birds make
their nests in, because she thought nests looked untidy.
'If I find you building your horrid untidy nests in my tree,'
she told the birds, 'I'll tear them down and break all
your eggs and eat all your babies! This is *my* tree—see?'
And she scratched her name on the trunk with her claws.

The birds were sad, because this was far the best tree
in that whole garden for nesting in. They twittered and
chattered, but they couldn't think what to do.

'Somebody think of a plan,' said a sparrow.

But nobody could. 'We *can't* think,' said a blackbird
sadly: 'We're too frightened of that horrid old cat to be
able to think, that's the trouble.'

'Well, if birds are frightened of cats, what are cats
frightened of?' asked a thrush.

'They're afraid of dogs,' said a linnet.

'Hooray!' said a robin: 'That wonder-dog who lives in
our village, I'm sure he would help.'

'You go and ask him,' the birds all twittered together.

So the robin flew down the village, and found the
wonder-dog doing his lessons as usual with the little boy
he belonged to. But when the robin started in at once
telling the dog about their trouble with the cat, that made
the little boy cross:

'Don't interrupt, you rude robin!' the little boy said.
'If you want to talk to my dog you must wait till his
lessons are over.'

So the robin hopped up and down without opening his
beak till lessons were done and the little boy had gone in
to dinner. Then he told the wonder-dog all about the
birds, and how the cat wouldn't let anyone build a nest in
her tree. 'So please come at once and frighten her,' said
the robin.

At first the wonder-dog didn't want to come: he was

too grand to think that chasing cats was fun, like ordinary dogs do. 'I can't come now,' said the dog, 'I haven't had dinner yet.'

'Then come this afternoon,' said the robin.

'I can't come this afternoon either,' said the dog. 'It's the little princess's birthday, and I've promised to go to the palace and show her my tricks.'

'Then come this evening,' begged the robin.

The robin looked so sad that the dog was sorry for him. 'O.K.,' said the dog, 'I'll come as soon as I get back from the palace. Six o'clock at the latest.'

'Promise?' said the robin.

'I promise,' said the dog, and laid his paw on his heart.

Just then the little boy came out with the dog's dinner, so the robin flew back to tell the other birds all to be ready by six o'clock.

When the wonder-dog had finished his dinner the little boy dressed him in his very smartest collar (which was made of bright red leather with shiny gold knobs) and sent him off to the palace by himself: 'Don't dawdle on the way,' the little boy said. 'And mind you don't get run over!'

When the wonder-dog got to the palace they took him straight to the little princess's room. It was piled with birthday-presents almost to the ceiling, but she was rather a spoilt child and didn't care much about any of them. When he got there she was busy pulling the legs off all her new dolls. All the same, she seemed glad to see the wonder-dog. 'Do you know how old I am today?' she asked him.

The dog didn't know, so he shook his head.

'It's a word rather like "licks",' said the princess. 'And rather like "fix" and "mix" and "tricks".'

That made it easy, so the wonder-dog dipped his paw

in the ink-pot and wrote a big figure '6' on the carpet in ink. 'Clever!' said the little princess and clapped her hands. But then she rubbed the wet figure '6' with her foot to spread the ink on the carpet and make as much mess as she could. 'You *have* made a mess!' she told him nastily. The wonder-dog had meant to lick his figure '6' off with his tongue while it was still wet: but it was too late now, and he said nothing.

'What else can you do?' she asked him.

There were lots of other tricks the wonder-dog knew how to do with the little boy he belonged to. For instance, the little boy would say the name of a city or a river and the wonder-dog would point it out on the map. Or the little boy asked him questions, and the wonder-dog shook his head when the answer was 'no' or nodded when it was 'yes'. But the little boy wasn't there, and you can't do that sort of trick with just any old ignorant little princess who doesn't know geography or arithmetic or anything much else. It would have to be something simple she could understand, so he started nosing about among the presents. He chose a policeman's uniform, a mouth-organ and a yellow tricycle. Then he put the policeman's helmet on his head and rode the tricycle round the room, blowing the mouth-organ as he went.

At first the little princess laughed, but she soon tired of it. 'Get off!' she said. 'That's *my* tricycle and I never said you could ride it. What else can you do?'

On the table was a vase of beautiful flowers. So the wonder-dog stood on his hind legs, picked up the vase with his two front paws and balanced it on his nose. Then he walked right round the room like that without spilling a drop. But the little princess threw a ball at him and knocked the vase off his nose so that it smashed on the floor.

'Stupid!' she said. 'Now I'll tell my mother *you* broke it!'

It wasn't his fault of course, but the dog looked ashamed and sorry all the same (as dogs often do if you scold them, even when they haven't done wrong).

'I know,' said the little princess, 'let's play hide-and-seek.'

So the dog shut his eyes, while the little princess climbed on the window-sill and wound herself in the curtain to hide. 'Cuckoo!' she called.

To a dog, even little princesses don't smell exactly alike. They don't just smell princessy in general, each has a special princessy smell of her own. So even with his eyes shut he knew at once where she was, though he pretended not to and seemed to be hunting all over the room. When he let himself find her at last, 'You *were* slow!' said the little princess. 'Now sing me a song.'

But singing of course was the one thing he couldn't do. 'Woof!' said the dog.

'Stupid!' said the little princess angrily. 'That isn't singing, that's barking. Sing properly!'

So the wonder-dog sat down with his nose in the air and howled, because that was the nearest he could get to singing. But this made the little princess even more angry. She caught him by his smart red collar with the gold knobs and dragged him into the next room.

'There's a piano in here,' she said, 'and you shan't come out till you've learned how to sing a whole song right through without any wrong notes!'

Then she slammed the door behind her and locked it.

The wonder-dog couldn't sing but he could play the piano all right—at any rate, simple tunes which he could hammer out with his paws on the keyboard. So he sat on the stool and started to play.

'*Sing!*' the little princess shouted through the key-hole. 'You shan't come out till you sing!' But still he could only howl. 'If you don't sing properly,' she shouted, 'you'll have to stop there all night.'

The poor dog didn't know what to do. He would never be able to sing in a million years. But he had to get out somehow because he had promised the robin to be there not later than six o'clock, to help the birds by scaring the cat—and he'd heard it strike 'Five' long ago.

He ran to the window, but it was fastened.

Then he saw a record-player, and that gave him an idea. He looked through the records till he found a song. As soon as he had started it he sat at the piano, pretending to thump it and silently opening and shutting his mouth. Next time the little princess peeped through the key-hole she thought it really was him singing at last.

'I knew you could sing if you really tried,' she said unlocking the door. 'Before, you just weren't trying.'

But when she saw the record-player she was even more furious still. 'You beastly cheat!' she cried, and tried to lock him in again. But the dog was too quick for her: he ran between her legs and bolted helter-skelter downstairs. In the hall the Queen tried to stop him, but he dodged past the Queen. At the front-door the King tried to stop him, but he jumped clean over the King. At the gate the soldier tried to stop him, but the wonder-dog tripped up the soldier and soon was right out of sight.

'I *must* keep my promise!' he thought as he ran, and sure enough there was the robin waiting for him.

'Quick!' said the dog, 'They're after me.' So the robin flew on ahead, and showed him the way to the garden where the other birds were all waiting too.

'This one is the cat's special tree,' said the robin: 'The one with her name on.'

'Yes, but where is the cat? I can't stop long or the soldiers will catch me!'

So everyone started to look, but they couldn't find the cat anywhere. 'She's bound to come back soon,' said the robin.

But the dog turned round to be off, and at that the birds all started talking at once—like this:

All together

  'Wait a minute!' sang the linnet,
  'What's the rush?' asked the thrush,
  '*Please* don't go!' croaked the crow,
  'Be a darling,' begged the starling,
  'Stop a bit,' chirped the tit,
  'Wait while we look,' cawed the rook,
  'She's coming—hark!' sang the lark.

'But I can't wait!' cried the dog, putting his paws over his ears to keep out the noise of them all: 'The soldiers will be here any minute!'

'Then we'll have to hide you,' said the robin. 'Just you climb up into the tree.'

So the wonder-dog climbed into the tree, and the birds all worked hard building a big nest round him to hide him. Rooks brought large twigs, blackbirds brought straws, little birds brought feathers and wool, and swallows brought sticky mud, and they all worked together without any quarrelling till in no time they had built such a huge nest round him that he couldn't be seen at all.

'Sh!' said the linnet. 'Quiet, everybody! I think I can hear the soldiers.'

So the soldiers came and searched all over the garden, but they couldn't find the wonder-dog anywhere.

'He certainly isn't here,' said the sergeant. 'Come on, we must look somewhere else.'

'What's that funny great bird's-nest up there?' said

one of the soldiers. 'It's big enough for an eagle or some-thing! May I climb up and see?'

'No you don't!' said the sergeant. 'What will the King say if we waste our time bird's-nesting instead of looking for the dog?'

So the soldiers all went away, and just then the cat came back.

When she saw that huge nest in *her* tree she was furious. 'Those beastly disobedient birds!' she said. 'I told them they mustn't, and now they've built the most horrible untidy nest there I've ever seen! I must tear it down at once.' So up she went. 'If I find someone in it I'll eat him all up,' she said.

'Grrr!' growled the dog, 'you'll eat *me* up, will you?' And he stuck out his head with bared teeth.

The cat was so scared she jumped straight to the ground and rushed out of the garden with the dog after her. 'Woof! Woof!' he barked as he chased her down the road. 'You just wait till I catch you!'

'Help! Help!' miaowed the cat, too frightened to turn round and spit at him. 'I never knew bird's-nests had dogs in them, I'll never dare touch one again.'

Just then she caught up with the soldiers. 'Save me, save me!' she cried, jumping on to the sergeant's shoulder and rubbing herself against his ear.

'What a nice friendly cat!' said the sergeant. 'That's an idea: if we can't find the dog, perhaps the little princess would like a cat instead.'

So the soldiers took the cat to the palace and tied a blue ribbon round her neck and took her upstairs to the little princess. 'What a *dear* little pussy!' said the princess, and gave the sergeant a chocolate.

Now she was a royal cat, the proud cat was even prouder than before.

When she saw the huge nest in HER tree she was furious.

At first the little princess was kind to her, and gave her cream and stroked her. But soon she started being even horrider to the cat than she had been to the wonder-dog, because she was that sort of child. She spilt ink in the cat's milk, and rubbed her fur the wrong way. She pulled her tail, and even held her under the cold tap.

If this had been just an ordinary little girl or boy (like you) the cat would have scratched her as she deserved. But this silly cat thought you mustn't scratch little princesses, so instead she just looked at her with angry green eyes full of hate and twitched the end of her tail and sulked.

Now that the cat had to live in the palace and was never let out it was fine for the birds, they could build their nests wherever they liked.

As for the wonder-dog, he went back to the little boy he belonged to. He showed the little boy the trick with the record-player, and soon the wonder-dog was famous for his singing all over the world. But sometimes he wanted a holiday, so then he would come back to the garden and climb the tree and sit in his dog's-nest and talk to his friends the birds.

The Palace on the Rock

THERE was once a King who lived in a one-roomed palace. It was on the top of a steep rock right in the middle of the town he governed. The top of the rock was so small that the palace covered it all, though the palace had only one room; and the sides of the rock were so steep that the only way to get up to the palace was to climb a rope.

Now this was all very well when the King was young; but as he got older he and the Queen had more and more children; and so, living together in one room like that, they began to feel rather crowded. The Queen was always telling the King he ought to build on other rooms to the palace; but when she said that, the King always asked her what she thought he was to build them on, seeing that the palace already covered the whole of the rock.

But all the same, the King thought there must be some way of doing it; so he sent for his Prime Minister. The Prime Minister was an old man with a long white beard, and did not much like scrambling up a rope to the palace; but when the King told him to, he had to, of course; so up he came.

'Look!' said the King. 'I've got sixteen children, and the Queen and I and all sixteen have to live together in one room. Just look what it's like!'

And indeed the room was in a terrible mess. The King sat on his throne in the middle with two of the older boys running clockwork trains between his legs. One of the little princesses was sitting in the coal-scuttle because there were no empty chairs left to sit on. The Queen had cleverly sewn the bottoms of two of the curtains to the tops, in order to make bags; and two more children were sitting in them, while the eldest prince shot at them with a water-pistol if ever they put their heads out. Two other children had climbed on to the King's desk and were busy emptying his ink-pot into the milk-jug. Far more children were sitting on the Queen's knees than there was room for; and the youngest of all, the baby, was asleep in the King's crown, which he had hung upside down from a hook in the ceiling.

The Prime Minister looked, and he agreed that something would have to be done about it; but the difficulty was to know what. So he told the King he would think it over.

'All right,' said the King, 'but think it over fairly quickly; and if you haven't thought what is to be done in a week, it will be the worse for you.'

So the Prime Minister slid down the rope again, and

began to think; but he couldn't think of anything. Then he remembered he had heard that down by the seaside a long way off there lived a wise old man; and perhaps that wise old man could help him. So the Prime Minister took his bicycle and began to bicycle to the sea. It was a long way, and there were many hills to go up and many hills to go down; and he was tired and out of breath when at last he came to the seaside.

There by the sea sat an old man mending some very large lobster-pots (which are traps for catching lobsters in). He did not look very wise; but since there was no one else about, the Prime Minister told him what the trouble was, and asked him what to do.

'How much money have you got with you?' said the old man.

'I've got sixteen pounds,' said the Prime Minister.

'That will be just enough,' said the old man, 'to buy from me these sixteen lobster-pots. And if you buy them I will give you sixteen big iron hooks as a present.'

'Why should I want your lobster-pots?' said the Prime Minister crossly. 'What use are they to me?'

'Think!' said the old man. 'After all, you *are* Prime Minister; you ought to be able to think out a simple thing like that! How many windows has the one-roomed palace got?'

'Sixteen,' said the Prime Minister.

'Well, then,' said the old man, 'that is just right. Hurry up, pay your money and take them away.'

So the Prime Minister paid for the pots and tied them all over his bicycle. Then he hung the iron hooks round his neck, where they dangled and jangled, and started to ride back to the town. It had been difficult riding down to the sea; but it was far harder and more tiring riding back to the town with all those pots and iron hooks. The Prime

Minister was tired and dusty and thirsty and wanting tea and dripping toast more than ever he had in his life before, when at last he got back to his home. But all the same he only made a hurried tea, and then climbed up the rope to the palace with all his pots and hooks.

When he got there, things were worse than ever before. If the children had been naughty before, they were twice as naughty now; and the King and Queen were nearly distracted.

'If you have got a really good idea,' said the King, 'I will give you ten sacks full of treasure.'

'Right,' said the Prime Minister, 'I have.' And he put all the pots down on the floor. He then put a bag of sweets in each pot. Then he went away as if he had forgotten the pots, and began leaning out of the windows, fixing an iron hook outside to the window-sill of each one.

Now it was not long before the children caught sight of the bags of sweets in the lobster-pots, because lobster-pots are made of a sort of open basket-work that you can easily see into. Each lobster-pot has a hole, of course, for the lobster to get in by; and once they saw the sweets inside, it was not long before the children were wriggling through the holes after them, one into each pot. Now, though lobster-pots are easy to get into, the whole clever-ness in making them lies in the fact that they are not nearly so easy to get out of; and once the children were inside them, there they were! They squawked a little and asked to be taken out.

'Not a bit of it,' said the Prime Minister. 'That's where you stay!' And taking all the lobster-pots one by one, he hung them on the hooks outside each of the windows.

'There!' he said to the King and Queen. 'Now you can have the whole room to yourselves, and a little peace at last! And yet the children will be quite handy to give their suppers to——if you remember to give them suppers, that is to say.'

'If they squawk too much I should just shut the windows,' he added.

The King and Queen were delighted, and thought they had got the cleverest Prime Minister that any King ever had (and indeed there are not many Prime Ministers today who can manage the same trouble so neatly). So the King gave him his sacks of treasure gladly, and the Prime Minister went home to have a second tea; and as he was eating it he looked out of his own window up at the palace, and thought how pretty the lobster-pots looked, swinging from all the window-sills, each with one of the pretty little royal children inside it.

The Cat and the Mouse

THERE was once a cat who had lost her spectacles, and she simply couldn't settle down quietly by the fire until she had found them. She hunted high and she hunted low, she miaowed here and she miaowed there, and poked her nose into all the most unlikely places; but she couldn't find them.

'I know I had them on when I was drinking my milk,' she said, 'but I *can't* remember whether or not I had them, the last time I went out in the garden!'

Now, what had really happened is this. The cat had taken them off while she was washing her face, and had left them lying on the floor. Then she had dozed off to sleep, and a cheeky little mouse had come out of his hole. He was a bold little fellow, and very hungry; so when he saw the cat was asleep, he took his chance and crept out into the room to look for some crumbs to eat. He did not find any crumbs, but he did find the cat's spectacles, under the table.

'Ha, ha!' he thought. 'This is where I win!' and seizing the spectacles, he raced back to his hole with them.

When the other mice heard what he had done, they were very glad and praised him a lot, and told him how clever he had been. 'And now,' they said, 'she won't be able to see to catch us!'

Meanwhile, the cat had at last made up her mind that she could not find them, and she had better just go to sleep and forget about them—and hope they would find themselves. But the cocky little mice poked their heads out of their holes and waggled their whiskers with laughing to think how they had got the better of the cat.

'Aha!' they squeaked to each other. 'Now she can't catch us!'

Cats never sleep very deep, and nothing wakes them so quickly as a mouse's squeak. The cat woke up at once. But cats are clever, and pussy was not going to show that she was awake. She just lay there with her eyes shut, listening to all they said.

'Ho, ho!' they said; and then they began to sing:

Ha-ha! Ho-ho! He-he!
Pussy's lost her spectacles and so she can't see!

Some of the mice had come out into the room and were actually dancing quite near to her. Then the cat pretended to wake up and be terribly worried.

'Oh dear!' she said. 'I can smell mice, but without my spectacles I can't see a thing!'

The mice scuttled off to a safe distance to watch her.

'I believe there is one over there,' she said, and pretended to make a clumsy pounce into the coal-scuttle, although she knew very well there was no mouse there at all. And then she actually bumped her head (on purpose) against the table-leg.

At that the mice were quite sure that she was almost blind without her spectacles, and became more cheeky than ever. They held hands and started dancing the Lambeth Walk all over the floor, teasing the poor cat and singing their silly song:

> *Ha-ha! Ho-ho! He-he!*
> *Pussy's lost her spectacles, and so she can't see!*
> *Pussy's lost her spectacles, and can't catch me!*

Meanwhile the clever cat still pretended to be nearly blind. The children's shoes were drying by the fire. She pretended to think that they were mice, and stalked them carefully, and then pounced. She actually picked up one of the shoes in her mouth and started to worry it. All the mice shouted with laughter. But the cat didn't drop the shoe: she ran round the room with it in her mouth. Then she dropped it right in front of the mouse-hole, so it blocked the door!

'Grrr!' she said in a growling voice. 'I'm blind, am I?'

And before they could collect their scattered little mousy wits, she pounced on one of them and gobbled him up. For the truth was that she only needed her spectacles for reading, and, in fact, she could see very well indeed without them!

The mice squeaked and the mice jibbered. They

bolted this way and that on their nimble little feet, but they could not get away from pussy—and before long she had had the biggest meal of mice she had ever had in her life.

Presently only one of them was left; and that was the cheeky little mouse who had stolen her spectacles in the first place. He alone did not seem frightened. He did not try to run away; he just stood in the middle of the floor and waited.

'All right,' he said, 'but you had better not gobble *me*!'

The cat pounced and held him down with one paw.

'And why shouldn't I gobble *you*?' she said.

'Because,' said the mouse, 'if you do, you will never get your spectacles back at all. I am the only living person who knows where they are.'

The cat had not thought of that, and of course it was true.

'Will you promise not to gobble me if I give them back?' said the mouse.

'I will promise,' said the cat, 'not to gobble you now.'

'That won't do,' said the mouse. 'You artful thing! You must promise not to gobble me *ever*, or else I know you will have no mercy once you get your glasses back!'

By this time the cat was so full of mouse that one more or less did not matter much. Besides, she really did want her spectacles, for as well as for reading, she needed them for fine sewing.

'All right,' she said, 'I promise not to gobble you ever. But you must promise, if I let you go, to bring them back to me.'

'I will,' said the mouse.

'Hand on your heart?' said the cat.

'Hand on my heart,' said the mouse, 'if you will let me get up to put it there.'

So the cat and the mouse both promised each other, each with a paw on his heart; and then the cat moved the shoe, and the mouse ran down his hole and fetched the spectacles.

And that is why in my house there is only one mouse, but he is the sleekest and laziest and fattest mouse you ever saw. He is never frightened of anyone, and will often sit under the table catching the crumbs as you drop them while you are eating your tea. But after he has had so much that he can hardly walk, it is quite common to see him sit down to warm his little pink nose in front of the fire, side by side with his dear old friend pussy!

THERE was once a motherly pig. She was nobody's pig, and so she did not live on a farm. She lived by herself in a large patch of gorse, and lived by selling gorse to passers-by.

One day an old man, very thin and dressed in black, came pushing his bicycle up the hill, so the motherly pig waved a nice bunch of gorse under his nose and asked him to buy it.

'How much?' said the old man crossly.

'Sixpence,' said the pig.

'I won't give more than twopence for it,' said the old man.

'The price is sixpence,' said the motherly pig very firmly, 'and you can't have it for a penny less!'

'Then you shan't sell any more gorse to anybody,' said the old man in a furious fury, and pulled a box of matches out of his pocket. Then he struck a match and set fire to the patch of gorse. The wind was blowing merrily, and soon the whole patch was ablaze. But the clever pig pretended not to mind.

'I don't care!' she said. 'I have got another patch of gorse over there, much bigger than this one!'

This was not true—there was no more gorse for miles around—but the old man believed her, and leaving his bicycle by the road he began running across the field to burn that too.

'Ha, ha!' said the motherly pig, and picked up the old man's bicycle. 'Now it is *you* who will walk home!'

She wrapped her blanket tight round her, and jumped on the bicycle and pedalled down the hill as fast as she could. But the old man was now even more furious than before. He pulled a little silver whistle out of his pocket and blew it. It was the kind of whistle that makes sea-gulls come. Sea-gulls came from the sea (which was not far away), and some sea-gulls who were feeding in a ploughed field came too; and on the old man's orders they all flew after the motherly pig on the stolen bicycle. They flew round her in circles and screeched like railway-engines, and flapped their wings in front of her face until she could hardly tell where she was going. So in a cloud of angry sea-gulls she free-wheeled down the hill, just missing a fat postman on one side of the road, and a thin signpost on the other side.

At the bottom of the hill there was a village, and the road went over a stream to get to it. But the motherly pig did not go over the stream. Alas, she rode straight into it instead, just because she could not see where she was going! When they saw that, the gulls were satisfied and flew back to the sea; and the poor pig scrambled back to the bank as well as she could, trailing her dripping blanket behind her.

Just then a kind-looking man with a big red face came down the village street; and he stopped in wonder to see the wet pig sitting so soused on the bank of the stream.

'Mrs. Pig,' he said very politely, 'I am sorry to see you have had an accident. Can I help you in any way?'

'Thank you,' said the motherly pig. 'It would be nice if I might get my blanket dry.'

'Certainly,' said the man with a red face. 'And won't you come home and have tea with me?'

So he wrung out her blanket for her and tucked it under one arm, and then took her hand; and they walked side by side up the village street to a shop at the end.

Now, the day was bright and sunny, so it will seem very strange to you what the man did next. Just before they got to his house he put up his umbrella and held it over the motherly pig's head, just as if it was raining. But the poor pig's head was so full of her adventures she never noticed how strange this was. She never knew that he was doing it so that she might not read the words that were written over the door of the shop:

J. JONES. PORK BUTCHER.

He opened a small side-door with a key, and they passed through into a cosy little sitting-room at the back with a large fire, and a pot of tea simmering on the hob.

'Sit down, sit down, my dear Mrs. Pig!' said the man in his kindest voice, rubbing his hands. 'Make yourself quite at home, and have an excellent tea!'

While he said this, he was putting on the table some hot buttered scones, and some dripping toast, and three different coloured jellies, and cake with sugar, and potted meat, and apples and oranges.

'Now pray do begin, Mrs. Pig,' he said, 'and don't wait for me; I shall be back in a moment!'

Then he slipped out of a door at the back of the room. And the motherly pig (who was very hungry) set to work to eat as much as she could. She ate the hot buttered scones, and the dripping toast, and the three different coloured jellies, and the cake with sugar, and the potted meat, and the apples and oranges, and she drank five cups of strong tea; and after that she felt better.

But soon she began to feel drowsy. So she sat down in a large armchair by the fire, and presently began to dose. From somewhere outside the door (where the man had gone) came the sound of a knife being sharpened.

'I wonder why that kind man is sharpening knives at this time of day,' she thought drowsily: 'and I wonder why he doesn't come back and have his tea?'

Then she fell sound asleep.

Suddenly she was woken up by the sound of a 'plump' on the table beside her, and looking up she saw a large tabby cat with a blue collar and a brass plate with his name (which was Robert) on it, sitting in the middle of the table. He had jumped in through a tiny window.

'Ugh!' grunted the pig in annoyance. 'Who let that horrid cat in? I always disliked cats.'

But the cat did not seem to mind that in the least.

'And I have always disliked pigs,' he said cheerfully. 'So now we are all square! But all the same, I have come to help you.'

'Thank you,' said the pig stiffly, 'I don't need help; I am very comfortable where I am.'

'*Comfortable!*' said the cat. 'Don't you know where it is you are? Don't you know who the man is who gave you your tea? *He is a pork butcher!* Listen, can't you hear him sharpening his knife? He will be back in a minute for a little free pork!'

When she heard that, the poor motherly pig shook with fright; so much that a rickety leg on her chair rattled on the hearthstone.

'Mercy me!' she said. 'However am I to get out of here?' And she ran to the door.

But both doors, she found, were locked: the red-faced man had been too clever.

Then she looked at the window which the cat had jumped in by. It was much too small for her to get out of.

'Yes,' said Robert, 'you have always disliked cats; but all the same, you will have to let me help you now! *I* can get away again quite easily'—and he turned round as if he were going to jump out of the little window again—'but you can't!'

'No,' said the pig, 'no, don't do that! Please come and help me to get away from here!'

'All right,' said the cat, 'I will, but you must keep your wits about you. We will wait quietly until the man comes back; and when he comes back I will upset the lamp as he is right in the doorway, and you must run between his legs as hard as you can pelt. Meanwhile, get back in your chair and pretend to be asleep.'

So the pig got back into her chair, and snorted and snuffled and snored as if she were sleeping deeply. Presently the door opened and the pork butcher came in. He had a large, wicked-looking knife in his hand, and a pleased smile on his face. But just at that moment the cat sprang at the lamp and suddenly everything was dark, and then with a frightful squeal the motherly pig sprang from the chair and pelted straight for the man's legs. His knife clattered on the ground, and he fell flat on his face on the floor. The pig wriggled between his legs and was out, and the cat was after her, giving the man a good scratch in passing.

'Quick, this way!' said the cat as they raced across the little, neglected vegetable garden at the back, and out into a lane that led back into the street.

'Come with me,' said the cat, and together they walked down the street, the pig still clutching her blanket (which now was nearly dry), till they came to a house right at the end of the village. The cat went straight up to the front door, knocked loudly, and rang the bell as well.

The door was opened by a little girl, who was dressed as a grown-up lady.

'Come in, Robert,' she said. 'Who is that you have got with you?'

'It's a friend of mine,' said Robert, 'who is coming to stay.'

'Oh dear, oh dear!' said the little girl. 'But we have no more blankets.'

'Never mind,' said the cat, 'she's brought her own.'

'In that case,' said the little girl, 'it will be fine. I am so glad you have come.'

The little girl lived all alone in this big house, and managed everything herself, but, as the motherly pig soon discovered, she had lots of people staying with her. She opened the door of the drawing-room, and there they all sat. There was a very old lion, and a young seal, two zebras and a foolish but good-natured young crocodile, and an elderly curate with patches on his elbows and knees, and two bears eating golden syrup out of the same tin. They looked a pleasant circle of friends; and there was no catch about it this time! This, at last, really was a comfortable, safe place to stay, the pig felt; and she was right. So she shook hands with everybody except the two bears (whose hands were much too sticky to shake). When bed-time came, just for friendliness they none of them slept in separate rooms, but all in a row in one big room. And the motherly pig, having no pillow of her own, shared one end of the one that the elderly curate slept on.

Indeed, this house was such a nice place to stay, and the little girl in grown-up's clothes such a nice person to stay with, that they all of them stayed on there for ever and ever and ever.

Evacuation

ONE day there was a war, and it was decided that all the animals should be evacuated. So they all came together to the railway-station and climbed into the train.

'Are you all right?' said the train. 'Then I'm off!' And away he went.

It was a funny sort of train, for it did not stick to the lines at all, but went just where it liked. If it wanted to go fast, it ran; if it wanted to rest, it stopped. The sun was shining, and when the middle of the day came the train felt hot; so it gave a loud whistle and ran into the sea to cool itself. While it was only paddling, all was well; but when it went in deep, the water, of course, came into the carriages and all the animals got wet. When that happened they hammered on the windows and cried, 'Hi, get on with our evacuation, you silly old train!'

So then the train remembered what he was supposed to be doing and hurried back to the shore. He took them up a long valley, and when he came to the end of the valley he stopped.

'This is where you get out,' he said; so out they all got.

'I wonder what happens to us next?' said the animals as they stood in a huddle on the platform.

'It's nothing to do with me,' said the train, and curled up for the night to sleep.

'I suppose we shall all stay with someone,' said the bear. 'I wonder who it will be?'

Clank, clank! Tinkle, tinkle! They could hear a funny jingling sound coming down the road, and presently round the corner came a fine tin doll. She had a tin feather in her hat and a red-painted petticoat of tin, and no one ever walked so stiffly as she walked.

Clank, clank! Tinkle, tinkle! There she was, in the station! When they saw her the animals all went shy at once and stood with their paws in their mouths, all except the bear. *He* wasn't shy.

'Where do we go?' he said to the doll.

'You are all coming to stay with me,' said the doll. 'The Billeting Officer says so.'

So then all the animals picked up their bundles and their gas-masks and started along the road with the doll. The road wandered away from the station towards the foot of a mountain; and the country got wilder and more deserted the farther they walked.

'*Where* are we going to stay?' said the bear.

'You are going to stay with me,' said the doll, 'as I told you, in my very comfortable home!'

'And where is that?' said the bear.

'Wait till we get there,' said the doll.

Before long the road came to an end at a field, a ragged sort of field with a large patch of nettles; and by the patch of nettles the doll stopped.

'Look!' she said. 'I hope you will all be comfortable. Come in.'

'Into what?' said the bear.

'Into my home,' said the doll, and pointed to an old tin kettle that someone had thrown away.

The animals looked at the tin kettle, and frankly they did not think much of it; but they were all too shy to say so. They just took the old paws out of their mouths and put in fresh ones. All, that is to say, except the bear. He did not want to be rude, but he felt he must say something.

'Do you think there will be room for all of us in that?' he said.

For the first time the doll seemed to consider the question. She looked at her home and she looked at the animals.

'Well,' she said, 'perhaps it will be rather a squash, as some of you are rather large. The Billeting Officer really ought to have thought of that when he said you were all to come and stay with me. Let's try the smaller ones first.'

'I think there might be room for *us*,' said three little beetles, and scuttled into the kettle. 'Yes,' they shouted from inside, 'it's lovely for us in here; just the sort of place we like.'

'And I think there ought to be room for me,' said a newt, peering down the spout. Presently he poked his head and shoulders into it, and with a wriggle of his tail he was inside too.

'Yes,' he shouted, 'it's fine for me in here too!'

'I believe there would be room for me,' said a fat puppy, not because there was any sense in the idea, but because he hated to be left out of anything. In fact, he was in such a hurry that he put his head in through the place where the lid should be and got it stuck there.

Now, if he had been a sensible puppy he would have waited until the others helped him get it out again, but as soon as he found his head was stuck he got in a fright and began to yowl. He tugged and he struggled, but he could not get it loose. He could not see, and he felt he could not breathe, and he was terrified out of his wits. So then he began to howl and his voice came out of the kettle all smothered and tinny, and that frightened him even more. So suddenly off he went galloping down the side of the hill as fast as he could pelt, the kettle still on his head; and as for the poor newt and the three beetles, you can imagine what a rattling they got inside.

They disappeared out of sight.

'So that's that!' said the bear. 'I wonder what next?'

'That's my lovely home gone,' said the tin doll sadly. 'You evacuees really are a bit rough and careless.'

'I think you had all better come into me,' said a curious, thundery voice. The animals looked round, but they could not see where it came from.

'Who is that speaking?' said the bear.

'It's me, the mountain,' said the voice. 'Look behind you.'

So they looked behind them; and, sure enough, a cave had opened in the side of the mountain—a pretty cave, with ferns all round the edge. The bear put his head in and sniffed.

'This is lovely,' he said; 'it couldn't be better! A nice dry cave with room for the lot of us!'

So all the animals trooped into the cave and then ran

out again to collect a pile of sticks. The glow-worm lit the sticks and made a fire, and the tin doll made tea for them all, and they all began to feel happier and soon forgot to be shy. The dormouse kept pushing the mole and giggling; and the cheeky little hedgehog (who knew he couldn't be smacked) called the tin doll 'Auntie Tinkle'.

'I wish I knew what had happened to my best friend, the newt,' said the mouse when he had finished eating an enormous tea.

'Here I am,' said a weak voice at the door of the cave; and the newt staggered in, looking much the worse for wear. He had got a black eye, and one of his paws was in a sling made of a blade of grass.

'Never in all my life,' said he, 'have I had such a shaking; but at last I managed to find my way out of the spout, and here I am.'

'Hooray!' said all the animals. 'We're glad to see you back.'

Just then the puppy came in, looking very ashamed of himself. He had got his head out of the kettle at last. The tin doll, naturally, was very angry with him.

'I should like to know what you have done with my house!' she said. 'It is all very well to turn it upside down,' she said—'one expects that when evacuees come—but to rush off down the hill with my house on your head, and finally to lose it altogether, that is a bit too much!' However, she could not remain angry with him long, and there was plenty of tea left for him too.

'Now,' said the bear, 'only the beetles are missing.'

'They will be all right,' said the zebra; 'beetles can look after themselves anywhere.'

He had hardly said that when, with a buzz and a whirr, the three beetles flew in through the cave door and flopped down by the fire.

'Quick!' they said. 'Some aspirin! We've got such splitting headaches.'

The tin doll seemed to have everything, even aspirin, and she quickly gave the beetles a dose. Then she made beds for the animals on the floor of the cave, each according to his size and shape, and they all settled down for the night.

'Well,' said the bear to the monkey, 'it's not so bad after all. I think it may be going to be fun.'

But the monkey said nothing. For the tin doll had taken off her red tin petticoat for the night, and he was far too busy licking the red paint off it to be able to speak.

A Sea Story

THERE was once a little boy who ran away to sea, and was lucky enough to get a whole ship to himself. She was a large sailing ship; but the little boy knew all about sails, and could manage her alone.

For some years he sailed about from island to island, chiefly visiting the parrots which lived on them and teaching them English. Whenever he landed on an island, too, he used to spend a lot of his time climbing the coconut palms (because these were tropical islands, with coconut palms and mangoes, and parrots and monkeys, and coral reefs and a bright sunny blue sea). When he was tired of one island he got back into his large ship and sailed to the next.

But after several years of lovely weather, one day the weather began to get bad. The sky grew cloudy and the wind began to blow too hard. Big grey clouds came rolling up from the edge of the sea, and went tumbling by overhead as fast as race-horses; and the wind grew stronger every minute. It grew stronger so fast that the little boy had no time to change his fine-weather sails for his bad-weather sails, and so all his fine-weather sails got blown away and torn to ribbons.

The little boy soon guessed that this was no ordinary storm, but a storm got up against him by some enemy who knew how to do wicked magic; so he thought he had better go down into the cabin and shut the door, and watch to see what happened.

Meanwhile the waves had got huge, and were tossing the ship about so much that he had to hold on to the arms of the cabin sofa or he would have been rolled off on to the floor! So he sat there, wishing for the first time that he was not quite alone on so big a ship.

'*Ha, ha! But you are not alone!*' said a hard, wicked voice suddenly behind him.

The little boy jumped up in a fright, and then saw a parrot sitting on the cabin shelf.

'Oh, good gracious!' said the little boy. 'You did give me a fright! I thought you might be the witch who has made the storm, and, after all, you are only a parrot off one of the islands!'

The parrot put her head on one side and scratched her ear with her claw, and gave a long, wicked laugh again.

'I am only a parrot, am I?' she said in a low, witch-like voice; and then to his surpise the little boy saw the parrot begin to change. She spread out her wings, and they changed into long, skinny arms; and her beak changed into a great hooked nose, and her bright feathers into just the sort of gaudy, tattered rags that a witch would wear.

'I *am* only a parrot, am I?' she said, jumping down off the shelf on to the cabin floor.

Now, when the little boy saw it was really a witch, he started to edge his way towards the cabin stove, because by the fire he kept his magic poker. It was one of the few things that he had brought with him when he ran away from home, because he knew it would come in useful some day, because he knew it hated witches and was far the best thing to fight them with.

The witch watched him edging along towards the stove.

'I know what you are after,' she said; 'your magic poker!' But, strange to say, she didn't try to stop him.

So the little boy gave a quick look at the stove; and then he saw why she hadn't tried to stop him. The magic poker was gone!

'Ha, ha!' said the witch. 'You don't think I'd come into the cabin with *that* there, do you? I've put it in a safe place, where *you* won't find it, young man!'

'Have you?' said a ringing voice from the cabin stairs; and to the surprise of them both, there came the poker hopping downstairs as fast as it could (being only one leg). 'You thought you had fastened me up safe, didn't you? But I know better magic than you!' And before you could say 'knife' the witch was yowling and running round the cabin, and the poker banging and bumping her wherever she went.

'Good!' said the little boy, full of pleasure. 'Hit her hard, drive her out!'

And that is just what the good little poker presently did. It gave her a couple of good bangs on the head, and then chased her up the cabin stairs and out on to the deck, thumping her all the time. Three times round the deck they ran; and at last the witch jumped over the ship's side into the sea.

Now, witches, you know, cannot drown; if they fall into the water they float, and I have no doubt that the witch this time did not mind in the least jumping overboard, because she thought she would float away to safety. But she had not reckoned with that magic poker. His head was small, but his magic was strong, and he thought of everything; so before he came down to the cabin he had wrought a wonderful change in the sea. He had changed all the waves into sea-dragons. These dragons were as good as they were beautiful; and the moment they saw the witch, they opened their foaming white jaws and swallowed her up, champing her to bits in their teeth.

When the little boy looked over the side and saw there was now no sea at all, but it was all turned to dragons who rocked the ship in their heaving about just like the sea did, and rolled their gleaming green sides and white crests almost like waves, he was astonished and a bit worried. For it was plain to him that there was now no sea at all. The ship was supported on nothing but dragons; and though he knew very well how to sail his ship on the sea, sailing his ship on dragons was something totally strange to him.

But things didn't stay like that for long. For now they had swallowed the witch, the dragons had nothing left to stay for; and they began to flounder away in different directions. When they did that, of course, the ship went down and down, until presently they were all gone, and she was resting actually on the sandy bottom of what had been the sea, but now was quite dry.

The witch jumped over the ship's side

The little boy was very excited at seeing the wonderful things on the bottom of the sea left all bare like this. Among them he saw the wreck of an old Spanish galleon, which had sunk long ago. It was covered with barnacles and seaweed, now already beginning to dry in the sun. Immediately the little boy climbed down a rope over the side of his own ship and ran across the sand to explore the wreck, and sure enough, it was full nearly to the deck with chests of gold and jewels.

So the little boy carried as many of them as he could (though they were frightfully heavy) across from the wrecked galleon to his own ship, and stowed them in the hold.

But when he had done that, he began to be very worried again. It was nice to have his ship loaded with treasure; but what was he to do next?

For his ship, like the wreck, was high and dry on the sand, on what had been the bottom of the sea; and how was he ever to sail it away, with no sea at all to sail it on?

So he wandered back again to the galleon, and went on exploring her; and presently he found a curious hammer hanging from a peg on the wall. There was magic-looking writing on it. The little boy could read that kind of writing, and what it said was this:

> *When the waters flee*
> *Strike the bottom thrice with me.*

So the little boy took the hammer off the peg, and jumped down out of the wreck and struck a rock once with the hammer. Nothing happened; so then he struck the rock a second time. Still nothing happened.

'It *did* say "thrice",' said the little boy to himself, 'and "thrice" means three times, so I will try again.'

So then he struck the rock a third time. Suddenly fountains started appearing out of the sand in all directions. Water began gushing up out of the ground, as if all the water-pipes in the world had burst; and in almost no time the little boy was up to his ankles. There was no time to be lost, so he began to run for his ship; but before he got anywhere near her, the water was up to his waist. Now, it is very difficult to run in water up to one's waist; but he did his best, and just before the water reached his chin he managed to catch hold of the rope which he had left dangling over the side, and so to haul himself up on board.

Meanwhile the water roared and swirled around, and rose faster and faster, and before very long he felt his ship begin to rock; and presently the water lifted her clear of the bottom, and she floated on top of the sea once more.

When his ship was afloat again, the little boy felt he had had enough of adventures for a time; so he brought out his spare sails, and rigged them in place of the ones which had blown away, and sailed back to the shores of his own home; and there he landed at last with all the gold and jewels he had got from the wreck of the Spanish galleon.

But he was even more careful to carry his magic poker safely ashore than he was with the gold and silver, for a poker which could thump witches like that on its own was not a poker to lose carelessly! It was worth more than all the gold and silver on the whole of the ocean bottom.

The Jungle School

ONE day all the animals in the jungle met together and decided to have a school for their cubs. It was the parrot's idea:

'You see how clever and big going to school makes men and women grow,' she said; 'perhaps it would do the same for us.'

So they all made up their minds to have a school; and next they had to decide who was to be mistress.

'I will be mistress,' said the elephant's daughter, 'because I can smack them with my long trunk.'

But when the other animals thought of their poor

little cubs being smacked by so enormous a mistress, they thought, No, she wouldn't do.

'I will be mistress,' said the monkey, 'because I'm so clever at stealing, and I will teach them all to steal as well as me.'

At that all the other animals were terribly shocked and angry, and chased the monkey away as far as they could.

'*I* will be mistress,' said the crocodile's daughter.

'Why?' said the other animals.

'Because I have nothing better to do,' said the crocodile, and shut her jaws with a snap.

So that was settled; and the next thing to decide was, *where* the school was to be. Some wanted it in one place, and some in another; it all depended on where they lived themselves.

'Let's have it up a tree,' suddenly piped the monkey, who had crept back again.

At that they were all angry with the poor little monkey again, and roared and hissed and bellowed at her so hard that once again she ran away in a fright.

'We will have the school in the middle of my swamp!' said Miss Crocodile, and again she shut her jaws with a snap.

None of the others liked the idea; but they hadn't been able to agree on any other place amongst themselves, and since she was to be mistress, they thought it really was for her to decide.

When the morning came, all the big animals brought their cubs down to the edge of the swamp. There they had to leave them, for the swamp was too quaky for the big, heavy animals to walk on: it was bad enough for the cubs, who were lighter. And even then they floundered and splashed about in the oozy mud, and actually had to swim in places; and some of them, especially the ones who hated getting wet, were rather frightened. But they were brave little cubs, and at last they all got to the crocodile's own pool right in the middle. Miss Crocodile had an old cracked bell in her wrinkled claw, and she was ringing it as hard as she could.

So all that morning she taught them lessons. But all she taught them was things about the swamp: muddy and oozy things, about rushes, and swamp-plants, and the sorts of slippery and creepy things that live in the swamp, and how to tell one kind of smelly slime from another.

Then dinner-time came, so the cubs all said: 'Please, Miss, may we go home now for our dinners?'

'No, my dears,' said Miss Crocodile, grinning with all her teeth, 'you will all stay here, for *my* dinner!' And with that she seized the poor little bear-cub, who was the fattest and most roly-poly of all, and gobbled him up!

When all the father and mother animals found their cubs didn't come home for dinner, they were worried; so they came down to the edge of the swamp and shouted. But Miss Crocodile didn't even bother to answer. So all the cubs called out together: 'We can't come back; she's eating us! She says she will eat us all up, one by one!'

At that the animals were terribly upset; but there was nothing they could do, because none of them were light enough to walk on the quaky swamp. They howled and they bellowed and they roared; but they couldn't go into the swamp to save their cubs. And they could roar their heads off, for all Miss Crocodile minded. But as for that little monkey, she didn't say anything. She knew it was one thing the animals weren't clever enough to manage on their own; so she hurried straight away through the trees to where there was a ruined palace hidden in the jungle, to see if there was anyone left in it who could give her advice.

When she got there the palace was all tumbled down and overgrown with creepers and trees; even more than she remembered it. At first she thought it was quite empty and dark; but she went on exploring, and at last she found one room where there was still an old man sitting. He was spinning cobwebs as cleverly as any spider.

So the monkey told him what was the trouble and asked him what to do.

'First you must learn to spin cobwebs,' said the old man.

So he gave her a jar of the shiny, gluey stuff he used for spinning them of, and taught her how to do it.

'Now,' he said, 'you must spin a rope of this stuff, strong enough for you to swing on, and tie it to a tree, and then you'll be able to swing it right out over the middle of the swamp.'

'But if I do that,' said the monkey, 'the crocodile will just snap with her jaws and gobble me.'

'You must sit in this magic basket,' said the old man; 'then she won't be able to see you, and you must give her this bowl of soup.'

'Is it poison?' asked the monkey.

'No,' said the old man, 'it is the very best soup. But listen. You must also give her this spoon to eat it with.'

'What then?' said the monkey.

'That's all,' said the old man. 'Go and do as I tell you.'

So the monkey took the jar of stuff for making cobwebs, and the magic basket, and the bowl of soup, and the spoon, and went back to the edge of the swamp. There she spun a rope strong enough to swing on, and tied it to a tree. Then she swung out on it, right over the middle of the swamp.

Miss Crocodile opened her jaws wide to snap up the

little monkey; but the monkey just slipped into the magic basket in time.

'Where are you?' said the crocodile crossly. 'I can't see you.'

'I've brought you this bowl of soup,' said the monkey.

'Is it poison?' asked the crocodile.

'No, on my honour it is the best soup.'

When the monkey said that, the crocodile knew it must be true, for the animals never tell lies, even to their worst enemies, when they say something 'on their honour'.

'And here is a spoon to eat it with,' said the monkey; and gave the crocodile the spoon.

So the crocodile took the spoon and began to eat the soup.

Now the soup was the most lovely soup she had ever tasted, and quite safe; but the spoon was a magic one. At first the crocodile ate her soup in a genteel sort of way, just tipping it out of the spoon into her mouth. If she had kept on like that she would have been all right; but the soup was *so* good she soon got greedy, and started putting the spoon right inside her mouth.

Now the spoon, as I told you, was a magic spoon, and as soon as she put it in her mouth the magic began. The spoon began to swell; it stuck between her teeth, and she couldn't get it out of her mouth again. Still it went on swelling, till it fixed her jaws wide open, and still she couldn't get it out.

Then the monkey started spinning cobwebs; and in about ten minutes she had spun the wicked crocodile up so tight in cobwebs she couldn't move; she couldn't even wiggle her tail.

'Quick!' called the monkey to the cubs. 'Come on!'

So one by one the cubs climbed into the basket; and because it was a magic basket, as each cub climbed in the basket got bigger, so at last there was room for them all. They were just going to escape, when suddenly they heard a little voice say, 'Wait for me'—and there was the bear-cub, just wriggling out of Miss Crocodile's open jaws! So then the monkey swung them all back safe and sound to dry land.

Then the animals were all glad, and were sorry they had been so horrid to the little monkey before, and wanted to make it up to her.

'I tell you what,' they said, 'now you shall be school-mistress instead, and you shall teach them whatever you like.'

'No,' said the monkey, 'I don't think I should really be a good schoolmistress, after all. But why not take them to the wise old man who lives in the ruined palace, and ask him to be teacher?'

So that is what the animals, very sensibly, did; and the old man said he would do it, and made a school for them in the ruins and taught them all kinds of things, many of which were magic. So all the cubs grew up wise and clever; so wise and clever that they were soon much wiser and cleverer than any of the ordinary men and women who lived in that country; much too wise and clever, by the time they were grown up, ever to let a crocodile be school-mistress to *their* children.

The Elephant's Picnic

ELEPHANTS are generally clever animals, but there was once an elephant who was very silly; and his great friend was a kangaroo. Now, kangaroos are not often clever animals, and this one certainly was not, so she and the elephant got on very well together.

One day they thought they would like to go off for a picnic by themselves. But they did not know anything about picnics, and had not the faintest idea of what to do to get ready.

'What do you do on a picnic?' the elephant asked a child he knew.

'Oh, we collect wood and make a fire, and then we boil the kettle,' said the child.

'What do you boil the kettle for?' said the elephant in surprise.

'Why, for tea, of course,' said the child in a snapping sort of way; so the elephant did not like to ask any more questions. But he went and told the kangaroo, and they collected together all the things they thought they would need.

When they got to the place where they were going to have their picnic, the kangaroo said that she would collect the wood because she had got a pouch to carry it back in. A kangaroo's pouch, of course, is very small; so the kangaroo carefully chose the smallest twigs she could find, and only about five or six of those. In fact, it took a lot of hopping to find any sticks small enough to go in her pouch at all; and it was a long time before she came back. But silly though the elephant was, he soon saw those sticks would not be enough for a fire.

'Now *I* will go off and get some wood,' he said.

His ideas of getting wood were very different. Instead of taking little twigs he pushed down whole trees with his forehead, and staggered back to the picnic-place with them rolled up in his trunk. Then the kangaroo struck a match, and they lit a bonfire made of whole trees. The blaze, of course, was enormous, and the fire so hot that for a long time they could not get near it; and it was not until it began to die down a bit that they were able to get near enough to cook anything.

'Now let's boil the kettle,' said the elephant. Amongst the things he had brought was a brightly shining copper kettle and a very large black iron saucepan. The elephant filled the saucepan with water.

'What are you doing that for?' said the kangaroo.

'To boil the kettle in, you silly,' said the elephant. So he popped the kettle in the saucepan of water, and put the saucepan on the fire; for he thought, the old juggins, that you boil a kettle in the same sort of way you boil an egg, or boil a cabbage! And the kangaroo, of course, did not know any better.

So they boiled and boiled the kettle, and every now and then they prodded it with a stick.

'It doesn't seem to be getting tender,' said the elephant sadly, 'and I am sure we can't eat it for tea until it does.'

So then away he went and got more wood for the fire; and still the saucepan boiled and boiled, and still the kettle remained as hard as ever. It was getting late now, almost dark.

'I am afraid it won't be ready for tea,' said the kangaroo, 'I am afraid we shall have to spend the night here. I wish we had got something with us to sleep in.'

'Haven't you?' said the elephant. 'You mean to say you didn't pack before you came away?'

'No,' said the kangaroo. 'What should I have packed, anyway?'

'Why, your trunk, of course,' said the elephant. 'That is what people pack.'

'But I haven't got a trunk,' said the kangaroo.

'Well, I have,' said the elephant, 'and I've packed it. Kindly pass the pepper; I want to unpack!'

So then the kangaroo passed the elephant the pepper, and the elephant took a good sniff. Then he gave a most enormous sneeze, and everything he had packed in his trunk shot out of it—toothbrush, spare socks, gym shoes, a comb, a bag of bull's-eyes, his pyjamas, and his Sunday suit. So then the elephant put on his pyjamas and lay down to sleep; but the kangaroo had no pyjamas, and so, of course, she could not possibly sleep.

'All right,' she said to the elephant; 'you sleep and I will sit up and keep the fire going.'

So all night the kangaroo kept the fire blazing brightly and the kettle boiling merrily in the saucepan. When the next morning came the elephant woke up.

'Now,' he said, 'let's have our breakfast.'

So they took the kettle out of the saucepan; and what do you think? *It was boiled as tender as tender could be!* So they cut it fairly in half and shared it between them, and ate it for their breakfast; and both agreed they had never had so good a breakfast in their lives.

Early Closing

THERE once was a funny old man who had seven
walking-sticks, and they were all of them different
colours. One was red and one was orange, and one was
yellow and one was green, and one was blue, and one was
purple, and one was white. Every day the old man went
for a walk, and every day of the week he carried a different
stick—the white one on Sundays; and if he met anyone on
his walk, what he always liked was for them to ask him
why he carried a different stick every day.

'So as to know what day of the week it is,' he would
answer; and then he went home very pleased with his
cleverness in having thought of such a thing.

But one day, when he was out on his walk, he met a small boy; and the small boy said, 'Good morning.'

'Good morning,' said the old man. 'Do you know why I carry a different coloured stick every day?'

'No,' said the small boy.

'It is so as to know what day of the week it is,' answered the old man, very pleased with himself.

'But *why* do you want to know what day of the week it is?' said the small boy.

Now, no one had ever asked the old gentleman that before, and he could not for the life of him think of a good answer. So he gave no answer at all, and hurried home not at all pleased with himself, wondering for the first time *why* he wanted to know what day of the week it was, and what good knowing it did him. He was still puzzling over it when he got back to his house.

He opened the front door. Now all the six walking-sticks, whose turn it was not, should have been standing in a rack just inside. That is where he kept them. But today they were not; they were standing on their points in the middle of the room, dancing up and down in a solemn dance!

It was a most surprising sight. Even the stick he had in his hand jumped away from him and joined the others on the floor, while the old gentleman stared in amazement at such an unusual thing.

Then the thing became more unusual still, because a strange and angry hissing sound began to come from the sticks—they thumped angrily on the floor, and before he knew what was happening he was running from his house and the seven walking-sticks were bumping along after him, chasing him as fast as he could go!

The old man ran as fast as he could pelt until he came to a river; and when he fell into it he did not mind very much, for he thought: 'At least the walking-sticks cannot walk in a river.' So he stood there, up to his neck in the water; and for a moment the sticks stopped on the bank. But then another strange thing happened. Instead of staying stiff and straight, they began to go all wavy—the seven coloured walking-sticks were turning into seven coloured eels before his eyes! When he saw that the old man knew he must swim for his life down the river; and off he went, with the seven eels swimming after him.

After he could swim no more he thought he had better land again; so he climbed up a bank and began to run across a field.

'At least,' he thought, 'eels cannot follow me on land.'

But he had hardly crossed a second field before he looked round, and what he saw was seven large coloured cockroaches, running behind him just as fast as he was running.

Now, just then he came to the edge of a wood; so he climbed the first tree he came to. 'If the cockroaches try to climb this tree,' he thought, 'I shall be able to knock them off as they come.'

But the seven coloured cockroaches did not try to climb the tree. They just stood round it in a ring at the bottom, and they began to dance. There was a red cockroach (you remember) and an orange one, and a yellow one and a green one, and a blue one and a purple one; and a white cockroach who seemed to be their leader. They danced faster and faster in a ring round the tree, so that soon all the colours seemed to get mixed and you could hardly see the separate cockroaches at all.

While the old gentleman up the tree was admiring this pretty sight, he saw a new strange thing happen. For the coloured cockroaches were now dancing so fast that soon they turned into flames; and as the flames danced higher and higher, presently the tree itself caught fire.

'What shall I do now?' thought the poor old gentleman. 'If I jump from the tree I shall be killed, and if I stay in it I shall be burnt alive!'

'Don't be afraid,' said a friendly monkey, who was sitting on the top of the next tree. 'Come over here.'

But the distance seemed too big to jump.

'I can't,' said the old gentleman sadly.

'Let me help you,' said the monkey kindly, and unwound his tail (which was very long) and reached it over towards the old gentleman. He caught it firmly in both his hands, and managed to swing across on to the monkey's tree. Together they watched the first tree burn with its seven different coloured flames.

'I see what your trouble is *now*,' said the monkey. 'But what I want to know is, how did it all begin?'

'It began,' said the old gentleman, 'with a little boy who asked me why it is important to know what day of the week it is; and I don't know the answer.'

'If you don't know the answer to that,' said the monkey, 'you will have to be chased some more; but you will know the answer in the end.'

And then, to the old man's horror, he saw the monkey, before his very eyes, change into seven monkeys; and instead of being just monkey-coloured, one of them was red, and one was orange, and one was yellow, and one was green, and one was blue, and one was purple; and a great white monkey was their leader. . . .

At that the old man climbed down the tree as fast as he could and began again to run for his dear life, with the seven coloured monkeys running behind him and growing every minute larger and fiercer as they ran.

At last, when the old man was so out of breath that he

could hardly run any more, he saw a cave ahead of him; so he crawled in through a door, and it clanged shut behind him, keeping the monkeys out.

'Just in time, sir,' said the voice of the owl that lived inside the cave. 'What can I do for you?'

'Tell me,' said the old man, 'why is it important to know what day of the week it is?'

'Why is it important?' said the owl in surprise. 'Of course it is important, because today is early-closing and if it had not been early-closing today the door would not have shut behind you as you came in; and if the door had not shut behind you as you came in, then the seven coloured monkeys would have caught you—and if they had caught you, I tremble to think of the horrible things they would have done to you!'

'Thank you,' said the old gentleman.

Then the owl let him out through the small back door of the cave, and he went quietly back to his home. On the way he met the same little boy. Just as if nothing had happened in between, he answered the little boy's question:

'Because it is most important,' he said, 'most important indeed, more important than you can possibly imagine, to know whether or not today is early-closing!'

Don't Blame Me!

THERE was once a young man called Simon, who
lived a long way from where he worked. So he
thought, 'If I could only buy a nice motor-bike to go
to my work on, that would be fine.' So Simon saved up
his money, till he thought he had nearly enough; and
one Saturday he went off to the street where second-hand
motor-bikes were sold, to see if he could find one to suit
him.

At almost the first shop he came to, there was a most
grand-looking motor-bike, almost new; and the price the
man was asking seemed much too cheap for such a fine
one. So Simon said he would buy it; but all the man said

was, 'Don't blame me!'—which seemed to Simon a funny thing to say.

Simon bought it, and rode it home; and it went sweetly and well, and he was very pleased with it. So on Monday morning he started out on it to his work; and as he went he wondered what the man who sold it meant when he said, 'Don't blame me!'

Simon knew soon enough, though; for as he was riding along a lonely piece of road, he felt the motor-bike beginning to wriggle under him, as if it was coming to bits. It wasn't doing that, but it was doing something far worse —it was turning into a crocodile!

When Simon found he was riding a crocodile, he was more frightened than he had ever been before. He was too frightened to stay on its back; so he jumped off, and began to run for his life with the crocodile after him; and at first he left the crocodile a bit behind.

But presently Simon began to get so tired that the crocodile began to catch him up, and he thought he would have to give up and be eaten. Just then he saw a donkey in the road before him. He managed to run till he had caught up the donkey, and then he said:

'Mr. Donkey, will you kindly give me a ride?'

But the donkey was a selfish one, not a nice donkey at all; and just because he saw Simon was really tired and needed a ride, he said, No, he wouldn't.

'You can jolly well walk,' he said. '*I* have to!'

'All right,' said Simon; 'then let me pass you,' for the road was rather narrow.

So the donkey let him pass; and Simon walked. Now that he had the donkey in between him and the crocodile he didn't feel quite so frightened; so he didn't trouble to walk very fast.

Presently the donkey said:

'Hee-haw! Hee-haw! Simon, Simon, will you walk a little faster? There's a crocodile behind me, and he's snapped off my tail.'

But Simon wouldn't trouble to walk faster, and the donkey couldn't pass him to get away from the crocodile; so presently the donkey said:

'Hee-haw! Hee-haw! HEE-HAW! *Will* you walk a little faster, *please*? There's a crocodile behind me, and he's swallowed me all but my head.'

But even then Simon wouldn't trouble to walk any faster; and then at last he heard the donkey say in a faint, small voice:

'Hee-haw! Hee-haw! I'm *inside* the crocodile now!'

So then Simon knew he would have to run again, so away he went for his life, with the crocodile after him. But because he had had a good rest, at first he left the crocodile behind; and also, of course, the crocodile had a heavy donkey inside him now.

Presently in the road ahead of him Simon saw a giant.

'Mr. Giant,' said Simon to the giant, 'will you kindly give me a ride?'

'Certainly!' said the giant kindly. 'Certainly, certainly, certainly!' So he picked up Simon and sat him on his shoulder, and went on strolling along the road, swinging his umbrella as he went.

Presently Simon saw the crocodile catching them up; but he didn't tell the giant, because he didn't quite know what to say.

'Ow!' the giant cried suddenly, and began to dance. 'I've been stung by a wasp!'

When the giant danced it was difficult for Simon to hold on; but somehow he managed, and looking down he saw what had really happened. It wasn't a wasp, it was the crocodile who had bitten the giant, and who was holding on to the seat of the giant's trousers like grim death.

But the giant couldn't see that, because it was behind him and his neck was stiff. He just kept on dancing and swishing behind him with his umbrella. And though Simon was sorry to have got the kind giant into so much trouble, he wasn't going to let go. He just hung on and hoped for the best.

At last, by great good luck, the giant managed to hit the crocodile with his umbrella. Now, giants' umbrellas are generally magic, and this one certainly was. For no sooner did it touch the crocodile, than the crocodile turned back again into a motor-bike, and just then Simon lost hold of the giant's collar and fell in the road a frightful thump on his head.

The thump knocked him silly at first, but presently he sat up and opened his eyes. There was the motor-bike lying in the road; a crowd of people was standing around.

'That's a nice motor-bike you've got,' said one of them. 'Do you want to sell it?'

'Yes,' said Simon.

'Then I'll buy it,' said the other chap.

'All right,' said Simon, 'buy it if you like, but *Don't Blame Me!*'

For Simon saw then what none of the others saw. He saw the motor-bike open its mouth and grin with all its wicked white teeth. And no wonder the motor-bike was pleased! For the young man who had bought it now was fat and juicy, and didn't look as if *he* could run an inch!

The Doll and the Mermaid

THERE was once a little girl who lived in a house by a river; and she had a wooden doll called Gertrude. Now though Gertrude was made of wood, still she had real hair and a real pink frock.

But as soon as the little girl got Gertrude, the first thing she did was to take off the pink frock and lose it in the apple-orchard; and the next thing she did was to comb Gertrude's hair. She used to sit and comb it for hours. She combed and she combed, and she tugged at all the tangles, till soon Gertrude had hardly any hair left.

Gertrude was very sad at losing her pink frock and losing most of her hair, and she decided to run away. But when she looked at the long black road, she thought how sore it would make her feet by the time she had run any distance worth while. So then she thought of the river. That would be a better sort of running away; she would get hold of something to use as a boat, and float easily down the river. Besides, she thought, people might be surprised to see her walking along the road without any clothes; but on the river it would look the best way to be.

The only thing she could find for a boat was a round white china bowl; so when it was night and even the grown-ups were asleep, she trundled the bowl downstairs and rolled it across the dark garden, and managed to float it on the river. Then she got in and pushed off.

It was a most exciting voyage; for the night was black as a cat. She couldn't see a thing. Sometimes the river bumped the bowl into the bank and set it spinning like a top. Sometimes she would go under a low branch of a tree, that nearly knocked her out of the bowl into the water. But at last morning came, and she was able to see where she was.

The river was much wider here, and the banks looked ever so far away. Ahead lay the sea; and already she could feel little waves rocking the bowl. But they were nothing to the waves she met with soon, once the bowl was out on the real sea! They spun it and rocked it and tossed it about, till every minute the doll thought she was going to be spilt out and drowned.

At last a giant big wave did come, which filled the bowl right up and sank it.

'Oh dear! Oh dear!' thought Gertrude. 'Now I shall drown for certain.'

But she didn't drown at all; and the reason was, because she was made of wood! She floated on top of the waves as light as a cork.

'What a good thing,' she thought, 'that I left my pink frock behind!'

The waves splashed and the waves dashed; but they couldn't sink the little wooden doll, who bobbed along merrily on top of them. Once she knew she couldn't sink, she thought what fun it was, and often rolled over and over just for pleasure.

Presently the waves washed her up to a rock; and on the rock a little mermaid was sitting, enjoying the way the waves tried to knock her off. But when the little mermaid saw the doll, she forgot all about her fun with the waves.

'Oh, how lovely!' she cried out. 'A doll which floats! A real mermaid's doll at last.'

Then she reached out and caught Gertrude up into her lap, and told her she had always wanted a doll and had often looked out for one when a ship was wrecked; but the only dolls she ever found were made of china or something like that, and sank to the deep bottom at once if she put them down on the water for a minute. So what use were they to her?

Gertrude was glad to be the mermaid's doll now, and they used to have lovely fun together, playing somersaults over the waves. Then, before they went to sleep at night, sometimes the mermaid told her stories about fishes and the sea, and what the Old Crab With One Claw used to say—for he was the wisest person on the bottom of the sea. And sometimes Gertrude told the mermaid stories about the land, and how the little rabbits used to come nibbling and hopping in the apple-orchard in the very early morning, and how the little girl had once polished her lesson-books with black boot polish to improve them a bit.

At last the mermaid said she would like to go and visit the land. She had often thought of it, she said, but was afraid of getting lost. But now Gertrude could come with her and show her the way.

So they swam together up the river till they came to the house where Gertrude used to live, and then they climbed out of the river on to the bank. It was night-time, and no one was about, so they thought they would go and explore the house.

'Come on,' said Gertrude, and started running across the lawn.

'I can't,' said the poor little mermaid; 'I haven't got any legs!'

And indeed, though she could dart about quick as a fish in the water, once she was out on the dry land she could hardly get along at all. All she could do was to drag herself over the grass with her hands, flapping her big tail behind her; and that was very slow. Gertrude kept forgetting and running on; but then the poor little mermaid cried 'Wait for me!' so sadly that Gertrude came back and waited for her.

When they got to the house Gertrude wanted to run all over it at once, to see if anything had been altered in any of the rooms, and to show it to her new friend; but the mermaid was so tired with flopping over the grass she asked if she couldn't stop and have a rest first.

So Gertrude helped her up on to the sofa in the draw-ing-room, and ran off to explore by herself. At last she came up to the room where the little girl was asleep. When she saw the little girl in bed asleep, Gertrude jumped up in bed with her as she had so often done before; and in a moment she had forgotten all about running away, and all about living in the sea, and all about the little mermaid she had left on the sofa downstairs! You may think that was very forgetful of her; but, after all, her head *was* made of wood.

When the little girl woke up in the morning and found her doll by her side again she was very pleased, and wouldn't put her down even to dress. She carried her under her arm when she went in to breakfast, and Gertrude felt like a cat when it is just going to purr.

But in the middle of breakfast, in came the maid with a most surprised look on her face.

'If you please, mum,' she said, 'there's a mermaid in the drawing-room.'

'Is it a big one?' asked the mother quickly.

'Oh, no, mum,' said the maid; 'it's only a little child-mermaid.'

When she heard that, Gertrude felt her cheeks go hot and red with shame for having forgotten. But it was against the rules for her to speak in front of grown-ups, so she couldn't say anything to explain.

So they all ran into the drawing-room, and there sure enough was the little mermaid, still fast asleep on the sofa.

'Oh, look!' said the mother. 'She's made the sofa all wet; and I *know* my best silk cushions are going to smell of fish!'

'What a darling!' said the father. 'I have always wanted a mermaid in the family.'

'I know you have!' said the mother quite sharply, 'but you shan't!'

As for the little girl, she didn't say anything at first, but just stood and looked. Then she said, 'I wonder what she weighs,' and tried to lift her to see if she was heavy.

That of course woke up the little mermaid, and she was terribly frightened until she saw Gertrude there with the rest. She flopped out of the little girl's arms on to the floor.

'Oh, isn't she sweet!' said the little girl.

And then the mother knew they would have to keep her, even if she *had* left a wet patch on the sofa; because it was two against one.

So the little girl and the mermaid were soon best friends. The little girl had always been fond of playing with water, and the mermaid could show her all sorts of new water-games she didn't know. By the time they had been playing a bit the nursery floor was nearly as wet as a lake; and every now and then water would drip through the ceiling of the dining-room below. The mother gave up even trying to keep the little girl dry. She let her get as wet as she liked all day, and only dried her with a towel at bed-time, and put a dry nightie on her, and put her in a warm dry bed for the night. For that was one thing that the mother was firm about. They could play together all day, but she WOULD NOT let the mermaid sleep with the little girl at night! When the last person had had their bath at night, the bath was filled up with cold water, and the little mermaid slept in that; which was really, of course, what she liked best.

So, though Gertrude began sometimes to feel a bit neglected by the other two by day, by night things were more as they used to be; she slept with the little girl as before, and was loved by her. But even then she did begin to wonder sometimes if it wasn't time the mermaid ended her visit and went back to the sea.

For it was quite plain, even to Gertrude, that the little girl and the mermaid now loved each other much better than either of them loved her.

Gertrude began
to feel a bit
neglected

And as time went on, things got even worse for Gertrude. They took to snubbing her when they played together, and to chucking her away into dark corners and leaving her there. When Gertrude had first been wrecked in the sea she had been glad she was made of wood because she floated; and now for the second time she felt what a good thing it was she was made of wood. For wood is hard, and not easily hurt.

She had really not noticed, before, that she was made of hard wood, while the little girl and the mermaid both were made of soft flesh. But now she began to despise them for it. If anybody chucked *them* about as she was chucked about, they would be covered in bruises and screaming the house down. But however hard they threw her about, they could not hurt *her*! Before, she used never to bother about having been made hard, but now she thought about it a lot. She did not even forget she was hard at night (as she used to) when the little girl cuddled her in bed. She did not say anything to the little girl, but she thought to herself, 'It's all very well: you bang me about by day and you think you make up for it by cuddling me at night! But you don't, and that's that!'

So things went on, all that summer; and when they were not playing in the sopping nursery, the little girl and the doll and the mermaid all played together in the river. That was the only time that Gertrude was really happy with them, because she could swim so much better than the little girl. And sometimes she and the mermaid used to swim off together, and it reminded her of the old happy days in the sea.

Moreover, when autumn came the river-water got cold. The mermaid did not mind this, and wanted to go on swimming there just the same; but the little girl said it was much too cold for *her*. So, quite often, the mermaid and Gertrude used to go off for a swim by themselves. One day, when they were swimming in the river, Gertrude said to the mermaid: 'Haven't you had enough of the land? How would it be to swim back to the sea?'

'What, now?' said the mermaid.

'Yes,' said Gertrude.

'No,' said the mermaid. 'In fact, I don't think I ever want to swim back to the sea again.'

That night Gertrude cried so much in the little girl's bed that it was almost as wet as if the mermaid had slept there after all.

But that same night they were all of them woken up by a strange sound outside.

It was a pouring wet and stormy night, with the moon shining now and then through racing clouds, and cold rain coming down in buckets. Yet besides the sound of the rain they could hear a strange slithering and sliding going on in the garden outside; and presently there was a big bump at the front door.

'Who is it?' said the mother, throwing up her window and looking out.

There in the garden she saw a strange sight. It was the little mermaid's mother and father, who had swum up the river and taken advantage of the wet night to flap their way across the grass to the house. And they weren't alone. There were seals with them, and porpoises, and even flying-fish skimming about amongst the trees; and an old walrus who reared up his head and coughed in a fierce sort of way. 'Ugh! Ugh!' he barked; and a sea-weedy smell blew in through the open window.

As well as moonlight there was lightning, and the sea-beasts glistened and shone.

'What is it you want?' the mother called out, rather frightened.

'We have come to take our little girl home,' said the merman in a hoarse, sighing voice.

'Yes, please let us have our little girl back,' said the big mermaid beside him, her beautiful long silvery tail quivering on the grass as if she were sobbing.

'She has visited with you long enough,' said the merman, and the walrus coughed again angrily.

'Oh, what a shame!' said the dry father indoors. 'I thought she would stay with us for ever.'

Then the bathroom window opened with a bang, and the little mermaid put her head out.

'I am sorry, Mother,' she said, 'but I am not coming back to the sea, not now or ever. I have quite made up my mind.'

A sort of strange sighing sound came up from all the sea-animals outside when they heard her say that, and an even stronger smell of fish and seaweed.

Meanwhile, of course, Gertrude and the little girl had slipped out of bed, and their window was open too, and they were watching.

'Well,' said the merman hoarsely, 'if our own child won't come back with us we had better have yours.'

'No, no,' cried the land mother indoors, 'you shan't have her!'

'Our own child or yours!' said the merman firmly. 'I have magic enough to make one of them come, but it is for you to choose which.'

The little girl ran from the bedroom to the bathroom and whispered to the little mermaid: 'Why shouldn't they have Gertrude? Why shouldn't *she* go back to the sea?'

'Yes,' whispered the little mermaid, and then shouted from the window to her father below: 'Why don't you have Gertrude?'

'Yes,' shouted the little girl too, 'do take Gertrude!'

'What a good idea!' said the little girl's mother and
father together. 'Gertrude would do splendidly for you.
She swims much better than our little girl does, and I am
sure she would like to go.'

'Wouldn't you, Gertrude darling?' said the little girl.

But Gertrude had never felt the wood she was made of
so hard before. She was hard right through, much too
hard to be hurt inside by anything they said, just as she
was too hard outside to be hurt when they threw her about.
She sat there stiff and not looking very pretty, and she
said nothing.

The merman looked at her and laughed. 'Not pretty
enough,' he said. 'You can't fob us off with her. Why,
look, she's got hardly any hair.'

When they saw that this idea was no good, there was
no doubt at all, of course, what the land mother would
decide.

'Darling,' she said to the little mermaid, 'it's been
lovely having you, but don't you think you had better
go home now?'

The little mermaid did not answer, but her green eyes
were very angry. 'If I do,' she said, 'Gertrude shall come
with me, too! Won't you, Gertrude?'

'No,' said Gertrude, 'I won't.'

At that the little mermaid was too angry to speak any
more. In dead silence she dragged herself on her hands to
the top of the stairs. She had become quite clever at doing
this; but now she was shaking with rage too much to be
careful. At the top of the stairs she slipped, and skiddered
the whole way to the bottom, where she landed with a
bang. But she was much too angry to cry. Then the chains
and the bolts on the front door mysteriously began to
open as the merman made his magic outside. The door
swung open of itself, and the little mermaid flopped out

amongst the strange sea-beasts on the wet grass outside. The cold rain was beating down, and it was wonderfully refreshing to her poor body, scraped and bruised on the dry, hard stairs.

'Good-bye,' barked the merman hoarsely.

'Good-bye,' said the mother mermaid.

But the little mermaid did not even call good-bye, for she was already so glad to be back with them again that she did not bother. She was rolling and squirming happily in a big puddle, and trying to splash water over her ears with her tail.

'Ugh!' said the walrus for the last time, spitting out a wind-fall apple he was tasting; and all the sea ones wriggled away through the darkness towards the river.

Then the little girl came to Gertrude and threw her arms about her. 'Darling Gertrude,' she said, 'thank goodness, I've still got *you*!'

'No,' said Gertrude. 'I'm tired of being anybody's doll! From now on I'm going to belong to myself.'

And then and there, before anyone could prevent her, Gertrude stumped down the stairs and out of the door, setting out into the wide world for the second time. But this time she never even thought of going the easy way by the river. She opened the little gate on to the black, shiny road, and strode away into the dark, her wooden feet tap-tapping on the hard tarmac; and she was glad to find that, although she walked all night, it didn't really make her feet sore at all.

When morning came she looked at herself in a bit of mirror she found by the side of the road, and a wonderful thing had happened. Her hair had grown again, thicker than ever! And she was even prettier now than when she was new.

Gertrude's Child

ONE night, Gertrude the wooden doll got furious because the little girl she belonged to was being unkind to her.

'I won't belong to you any more!' said Gertrude: 'I don't want to belong to anyone, only myself.'

So Gertrude ran away. I mean, she ran *right* away— right along the main road out into the world on her own; and the night was dark.

Gertrude was glad she was made of wood and not easily hurt, for her hard little wooden feet went clickety-clop on the hard road without any shoes yet didn't get sore. She was painted with oil paint, too, so the rain just ran off her. Also, wooden dolls don't need any dinner. At dolls' parties they eat what you give them of course, and enjoy it; but in between parties wooden dolls need eat nothing at all.

Nearly Gertrude felt sorry for the little girl she had run away from, for being made of that soft stuff all children are made of which scratches and bruises so easily, and falls ill ... But no, for Gertrude was wooden and hard right through, and *couldn't* be sorry for someone who'd been unkind to her. 'I hope she falls down and bleeds!' said Gertrude to herself: 'That's what she deserves!'

Then daylight came, and the sun came out and dried Gertrude, and made the paint on her hard wooden shoulders smell good. She began to sing (quite loud, though her voice was woody).

But all that day Gertrude met no one at all on the road, and began to feel lonely. She thought that it might be nice after all to have a friend—not a soft one of course, but a sensible hard one like herself. So Gertrude made up a story in her head about another wooden doll, and pretended this other wooden doll was walking beside her and talking to her (but it wasn't, of course: she was quite alone really).

When it got dark again Gertrude looked up at the face of the moon, because it was the only face round there to look at. 'You're not much company, Moon!' said Gertrude. 'But that's all right because I don't really *want* company.' (This wasn't quite true, though she wished it was.)

But she had not walked very much farther when she came up behind an old man carrying a load on his back. The old man took her hand, and they walked along together hand-in-hand for a while. But he didn't say anything to her—not a word. 'Very old men never do know what to say to dolls,' Gertrude told herself.

But at last the old man stopped outside a cottage, and then he did speak to her: 'Would you like a little girl of your own?' he asked Gertrude.

'No!' said Gertrude: 'I don't want to belong to any little girl again, ever!'

'You don't understand,' said the old man: '*You* wouldn't belong to *her*, *she* would belong to *you*.'

'I don't see how . . .' said Gertrude.

'Come round to my shop in the morning and I'll explain,' said the old man. 'You see, I sell little girls in my shop. And little boys too, if you'd rather.'

'Who *on earth* wants to buy them?' asked Gertrude, astonished.

'I'll tell you tomorrow,' said the old man. 'Good night for now!'

He went into his cottage and shut the door.

Gertrude walked on. She wondered who he sold little girls to. Suppose she bought one: would a little girl turn out more trouble than she was worth? Certainly no child could be as good company for Gertrude as a real doll would be—but perhaps dolls couldn't buy *dolls*. . . .

Gertrude had felt very lonely while it was dark, but when morning came she did not feel quite so lonely and so she forgot the idea of buying herself a child. She was thinking of something quite different, when all of a sudden she saw the old man standing at the door of a small road-side shop.

Seeing him made her remember. 'Hullo!' she said: '*Now* tell me who buys your children?'

'Oh, mostly dolls like yourself do,' said the old man: 'Or else other toys. And puppies of course; but puppies don't often have money enough—they spend it too fast. Sometimes I sell one to a pony. But ponies seldom want children very much—they're too happy playing about by themselves. As for kittens . . . I don't really like selling children to kittens, because kittens can be so cruel!'

'What kind of children do you sell?' asked Gertrude.

'I sell all kinds and all ages,' said the old man. 'Fat ones and thin ones, pretty and plain, good ones and naughty ones. You'll see some in the shop-window here, but I've lots more inside.'

Gertrude looked in the window. It was got up to look like a Christmas party. Children of all sizes were sitting about in their very best clothes. Little girls had no creases at all in their pretty dresses: little boys had clean hands, and their hair was all smarmed down and oiled. The children looked stiff and shy, like people having their photographs taken. Not one of them wriggled: being stared at in a window like this made them even too shy to pull the crackers they held in their hands.

When she saw them, a great longing came over Gertrude to have one of her own: 'Oh, I *must* have one of those grand-looking ones!' said Gertrude.

'Come and look at the others inside before you make up your mind,' said the old man, and led her into the shop.

Inside, Gertrude saw piles of children all over everywhere—every kind of child you could think of: as well as English ones there were Spanish and Russian and Dutch, and some Africans, and a special shelf of Chinese ones, and even an Indian pair who were brown.

There was, too, one very shining and precious child in a box by herself, who lay very still. 'That's a *most* beautiful one,' Gertrude whispered.

'Yes, but she wouldn't be any good to you,' said the

old man very sadly: 'She doesn't move at all now. Her eyes won't open any more.'

Still, there were plenty of children to choose from. Some were sitting in rows on the shelves (which were too high for them to climb down without help). Because it was the middle of the morning they were all eating biscuits and drinking glasses of milk.

'Can they sing?' Gertrude asked.

'Of course they can sing!' said the old man. He waved his hand, and the children stopped munching their biscuits and sang Gertrude's favourite song.

'Now that you've seen them all you'd better choose one,' said the old man.

'May I feel them first?' asked Gertrude, because she couldn't believe they were real.

'Yes, if your hands are clean,' said the old man.

So Gertrude poked them with her hard wooden fingers and felt their ribs, and the ones who were ticklish giggled and squealed no end. 'Now you've poked them enough,' said the old man. 'Hurry up and choose, before you've made them all spill their milk.'

Gertrude liked nearly all of them. But there was one little girl she was certain sure she would best like to have for her own. This little girl was about six years old, and a bit thin: she had curly yellow hair and a pretty pink dress, and short white socks, and a happy look in her eye.

'If she's naughty,' thought Gertrude, 'I'll smack her and smack her and smack her! That's the only way of making them good,' thought Gertrude (since that was how she'd been treated herself).

But the old man seemed to know what she was thinking, and said to Gertrude: 'If I sell her to you, you must promise to be kind to her! Remember, children aren't hard like you wooden dolls. If you drag *children* by the leg head-down through bushes, they get scratched and bruised. If you drop them from the top of the stairs, they break their necks. If you take their clothes off and leave them out in the cold, they get ill. If you forget to feed them they die, just like animal pets do.'

'Oh, I promise to be kind to her,' said Gertrude: 'But you said about her clothes—do you mean her clothes really take off?'

'Of course they do!' said the old man: 'But remember what I said about being kind to her, and not letting her catch cold.'

'Yes yes!' said Gertrude, even more hurriedly. Quickly she paid the price, then caught her little girl by the arm and ran out of the shop with her.

'Don't forget to give her her dinner!' the old man shouted after them.

'Good-bye! Good-bye, child!' called all the children left on the shelf (all except the very beautiful one in the box whose eyes wouldn't open).

Gertrude was delighted with her child. At first all she wanted to do was to walk up and down the street, leading her child by the hand.

Gertrude saw other dolls and puppies and people like that taking *their* children out for a walk, and she hoped they were jealous of her for having such a pretty one. But soon she got tired of this, and then she began to remember all the many things you have to do when you have a child to look after: all the washing and minding and mending for her, and feeding and cleaning and cooking and catching and combing and teaching and sewing and cuddling and bandaging and reading aloud. You couldn't do all that just wandering around: it meant having a home.

'There's a house just round the corner from here we could live in,' said the child.

'And I'm going to call you Annie,' said Gertrude. 'You can't manage without a name.'

'Good!' said the child, 'I'm Annie, then.' And together they went in through the gate.

Inside the gate, in front of the house there was a beautiful garden, with flowers growing. But round the back there was an orchard, so they went straight there to explore it.

Suddenly Gertrude began wondering if what the old man had said was true and Annie's clothes really did come off: for she feared that they might be sewed to her skin, the way a doll's clothes sometimes are. She took Annie's pretty pink dress off, just to find out. . . . 'I'll remember to put it on her again *for certain*,' thought Gertrude.

Then she went on undressing Annie, dropping her clothes on the ground. 'Stop undressing me, it's c-c-cold!' said Annie.

'Nonsense!' said Gertrude. 'I must just find out if they *all* really unbutton.'

Annie tried to run away, but Gertrude kept catching her and taking off one thing more. Annie was so hard to catch that Gertrude kept dropping the clothes all over everywhere. The sun had gone in now, and it started to snow. 'Oooooo! I'm so *cold*!' shivered Annie.

'Nonsense!' said Gertrude (who never felt cold herself, of course). 'You're not a bit cold really, so don't make a fuss!' And she undressed Annie completely.

When there were no more clothes to take off, Gertrude left Annie and started making snowballs to throw at the birds. Annie sat on the ground all bare, and shivered and howled. Annie couldn't find her clothes to put on again because they were all buried by now in the falling snow.

But at last Gertrude got tired of snowballing the birds. 'Come on in. Don't sit there dawdling around,' she said to Annie. 'Come into the house!'

'Is it dinner-time yet?' asked Annie, her teeth chattering. 'It feels like it must be.'

'*Dinner?*' said Gertrude: 'Yes—later on. But first I must cut your hair.'

So Gertrude took a pair of scissors and began cutting Annie's lovely hair. But she soon found she had cut off too much on one side, which meant she then had to cut more off the other to match; and so it went on, till Annie's head had hardly any hair left. Then Gertrude was sad, because nothing was left to cut.

'Is it dinner-time *now?*' asked Annie, when her hair was all gone.

'No, you bad child! It's your bed-time,' said Gertrude.

It wasn't really anywhere near bed-time, but Gertrude was cross with Annie for looking like a scarecrow with her hair all cut off. Besides, she wanted to be free of the child for a bit, to think her own thoughts. So she filled the bath with warm water, dropped Annie in as quick as she could, and then went away and left her there in the bath!

Gertrude went off to explore the house. It was a wonderful house, with cupboards everywhere—and every sort of thing you could want was there in the cupboards, all ready to hand! Gertrude spent hours and hours exploring the house, and came at last to the kitchen. There on the table was a whole pound of sausages. 'I think I'll have some supper, for once,' said Gertrude to herself. So she cooked the sausages, then sat down in front of the kitchen stove and ate them all up.

As she finished the last of them Gertrude felt sleepy, so went straight upstairs and got into a bed. She had

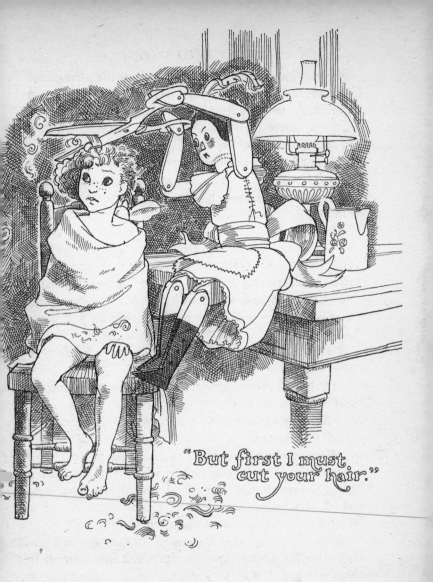

"But first I must cut your hair."

forgotten all about poor Annie, left sitting there in the bath!

It was not till Gertrude was just dropping off to sleep that at last she remembered Annie. 'Poor Annie!' she

173

thought: 'How horrible, having to pass the whole night in the bath!' But it was very, very dark; and Gertrude didn't want to get out of bed. 'Perhaps she *likes* sleeping in baths better than beds,' Gertrude told herself. 'Yes, I'm sure Annie would *rather* stop all night in the bath. . . .'

Yet Gertrude knew in her heart that this couldn't be true. Only a fish (or a mermaid) could like sleeping in water all night. 'Come on, Gertrude!' she said to herself: 'Up you get!'

Gertrude jumped out of bed, and taking two torches (one for each hand) she ran to the bathroom. There was Annie, still sitting in the water, which by now was quite cold. Annie looked very sad, and her teeth were chattering. But Gertrude soon had her out of the water, and dried her with a towel, and carried Annie off with her to bed.

'Darling Annie!' said Gertrude in bed, putting her hard wooden arm round Annie's neck.

'Darling Doll!' said Annie. 'How kind to me you are!'

And so they both fell asleep, with their arms tight round each other.

When they woke in the morning, Annie had a cold in her head. Her nose was red, and dripping. She had no hair, and no clothes. She didn't look pretty now, as she had in the shop.

'I must make you some new clothes, now that you've lost your others,' said Gertrude. So she took the cloth off the table and cut it up and made it into clothes. But they were not very nice clothes, because Gertrude had never learned sewing. Indeed Gertrude had hardly any idea at all about how to make clothes. All the same, Annie seemed just as pleased as if her tablecloth dress was the most beautiful dress in the world.

'What are we going to do today?' asked Annie, admiring her new dress in the mirror.

'We're going to have a party,' said Gertrude: 'It's your birthday today! But first you have to be smacked for losing your clothes.'

It wasn't fair for Annie to be smacked, because it was Gertrude herself who had lost them. But Annie just said, 'I'm sorry, and I won't do it again.'

' "Sorry" is not enough! You'll have to be punished as well,' said Gertrude.

Annie howled when Gertrude smacked her (and so would *you* howl if somebody smacked you with hard wooden hands!). But Gertrude didn't know how much she was hurting, of course.

'Stop crying at once, now!' said Gertrude as soon as the smacking was over. 'It's time to get ready for the party.'

So all the morning they made cakes and baked them, and put icing on top to look like flowers. Then they set out the candles, and hung up red paper streamers to make the room look pretty, and phoned people asking them to come.

At three in the afternoon they heard someone knock on the door. Annie wanted to open it. But Gertrude sent her up to the bathroom to wash her hands. 'Wait in the bathroom till I come up to see you're really clean!' Gertrude called up the stairs after Annie, and went to open the door herself.

It was the first guest come for the party. There on the step stood a big teddy-bear, leading a very small boy by the hand.

'Come in, and be a good boy,' the toy bear whispered to his little boy as Gertrude let them in. 'And remember you mustn't shout for things: you must wait till the cakes are offered you, and say "Thank you".'

'Yes, Uncle Teddy,' said the little boy (but he wasn't really listening).

Next came a rocking-horse. *He* had to be helped up the steps by the three children he had brought with him. One pulled in front and two pushed behind. The children looked very proud to belong to such a fine horse.

Then came a small dumpy doll, dragging with her quite a big lanky schoolgirl. 'Surely you're too old to belong to a doll!' Gertrude burst out when she saw her.

'That's what *I* think,' said the big girl: 'But she has had me since I was tiny, years ago—and now she won't believe I'm almost grown-up!'

'Don't talk so daft, Miss Theodora!' said the doll severely: 'You're no more than a big baby still—and don't you forget it! Now, you behave nicely or I'll punish you!'

The little doll looked so fierce that the big girl was afraid of her: 'S-sorry,' the big girl said, and put her thumb in her mouth.

Next came a puppy, dragging a small boy behind him on a rope. The puppy marched straight in without even a 'How-d'you-do' to Gertrude and jumped up into a chair at the table where the food was spread out. The little boy tried to climb up beside him, but 'Lie down!' barked the puppy to the little boy, 'Or you'll be tied up outside and not have any cakes at all!'

So the little boy crept under the table, and curled up by his master's chair.

Then all the dolls and toys climbed into chairs. But their children were not allowed at table at all! The children had to sit in a row on a bench in the corner: only the puppy's little boy was allowed to stay curled up on the floor, chewing his rope.

'You be good!' shouted all the dolls and toys to the children together. 'Then perhaps we'll let you have some bread-and-butter, if by the time we've finished the cakes we can't eat any more ourselves.'

'I hear you have a child too, haven't you?' the teddy-bear asked Gertrude with his mouth full of chocolate biscuit: 'Where is she?'

Goodness gracious! Once again Gertrude had altogether forgotten Annie, after sending her up to the bathroom to wash her hands!

But then Gertrude looked round the party, and saw all those proud toys with their charming fashion-magazine children, in their very best clothes, sitting so good and neat in the corner; and Gertrude felt ashamed of Annie with her tablecloth dress, and no hair, and her nose all runny. Gertrude couldn't bear all these grand toys to see Annie, or even to know she owned a child who looked so common and shabby.

Then Gertrude told a lie: 'Annie's been naughty,' she said. 'I had to send her to bed for a punishment.' (Poor Annie! And this was *her* birthday party, after all!)

'Never mind,' said the teddy-bear: 'It's probably just as well. If she's a naughty child I'm sure I don't want *my* little boy to meet her. She might make him naughty too.'

'Quite right!' said all the other toys together: 'I'm sure if she's naughty we none of us want *our* children to play with her!'

Gertrude began to feel she wasn't liking this party any longer. . . .

Just then they heard a scream from the garden outside, and the puppy's little boy got up and ran to the window, trailing his rope. 'I say!' he cried out, very excited: 'It's a—'

'Lie down!' barked the puppy. 'And don't speak till you're spoken to!'

'But it's a—'

'Do as you're told!' yapped the puppy: so the little boy became quiet.

'But I saw it too!' said one of the other children: 'It was—'

'Be quiet or I'll rock on you!' said the rocking-horse, furious.

'I *won't* be quiet!' said the child bravely. 'There's a lion in the garden, and he has caught Gertrude's child and is eating her up!'

'Well, well,' said the teddy-bear: 'What a *very* naughty little girl she must be, to need to be eaten by a lion!'

'It sounds horrid and vulgar,' said the prim little doll that the big girl belonged to: 'I'm sure I don't want to hear anything about it till I've finished my tea.'

'Quite right!' said the teddy-bear: 'It's spoiling my appetite too! Let us talk of pleasanter subjects.'

'I think I would like some more ice-cream,' said the rocking-horse: 'If Annie is being eaten by a lion there's no use saving any for *her*.'

But Gertrude sprang to her feet in a blazing rage. 'You brutes and horrors and pigs!' Gertrude cried: 'You're not going just to sit there and *let* her be eaten, are you?'

'It's none of *our* business,' said the party.

But Gertrude didn't wait.

She seized the teapot in one hand and a spoon in the other and jumped out of the window. There was the lion, skulking about in the garden with Annie in his mouth, looking for a comfortable place to lie down and eat her.

'Drop her!' cried Gertrude: 'Put my child down at once, Sir!'

But the lion only growled, and flicked his tail.

Poor Annie was very frightened, and not screaming now. The lion was huge. But Gertrude didn't wait for a moment: she threw the teapot full of hot tea right in his face and sprang at him with the spoon.

The lion roared with pain from the hot tea and dropped Annie—but instead, he seized Gertrude's arm in his teeth.

'Run, Annie!' cried Gertrude: 'Run in the house and be safe!'

'I *won't* run and leave you to be eaten!' cried Annie.

Annie tore up handfuls of snow and started pelting the lion to make him let go of Gertrude's arm, but— scrunch! The lion had bitten Gertrude's arm right off.

'*Ugh!*' growled the lion, 'she's only made of wood after all, and I don't like eating wooden people one bit!'

Meanwhile all the children had jumped out of the window (leaving the toys to finish the ice-cream) and were pelting and booing the lion.

'I suppose they're all made of wood too, and don't taste as nice as they look,' grumbled the lion, trying with his claws to get the wood splinters out of his teeth.

Just then a big ball of snow hit the lion slap in the eye. He dropped Gertrude's arm on the ground, and ran right away, and was gone.

But Gertrude had lost her arm. 'Oh, *poor* Gertrude!' said Annie.

'Never mind,' said Gertrude bravely. 'It doesn't hurt *too* much.'

'How lucky you're made of wood and don't feel things the way we do!' said Annie.

'Y-y-yes,' said Gertrude, trying her best not to cry.

But it was hard for her not to cry, for something strange was happening to Gertrude: never in all her life had she felt so *un*wooden as now! Indeed her gone arm was hurting her horribly—almost as if she wasn't a doll, but a person.

Then the brave little boy who belonged to the rocking-horse picked up Gertrude's chewed arm and examined it. 'I think I can mend this,' he said, 'with my carpentry tools.' So he mended Gertrude's arm and fixed it on again, and the children all cheered.

Then the children went back indoors, because the toys they belonged to (and also the puppy) were calling angrily from the window. But Gertrude and Annie stopped outside together.

'Annie!' said Gertrude; 'Listen. I think it's a stupid idea, dolls *having* to belong to children or children to dolls. Why can't they just be friends?'

'And both look after each other?'

'Yes. Anyway, that's how *we* are going to be from now on,' said Gertrude: 'You won't belong to me and I won't belong to you—not neither. So, now let us start on our travels!'

Then Annie and Gertrude put their arms round each other's waists, and started along that hard black road together. And the curious thing was this: Annie thought Gertrude's arm now felt soft, and warm—almost like the arm of another child: while Gertrude found Annie's arm comforting and *strong*—almost as if it too were a wooden one.

That's all about Gertrude and Annie for now. . . .

*We hope you have enjoyed this book.
There are more than 1000 others to choose
from in Puffins, and some of them are
described on the following pages.*

Goldenrod

Jim Slater

As William grew up he found he had some very special powers. First of all, he could hear what people were saying although they were a long way off, and then an Indian fakir taught him how to concentrate his mind so that he possessed in a single minute all the strength he usually had in an hour. These powers, and a third, remained with William after an operation had made it possible for him to see. His specially-trained guide-dog, Rajah, stayed with him, too, as did his nickname, Goldenrod.

As it happened, William desperately needed all his powers – and the help of Rajah – when hijackers seized control of an aeroplane in which he was travelling high above the deserts of Saudi Arabia.

A Traveller in Time

Alison Uttley

A young girl, Penelope, living in her Great Uncle's remote Derbyshire farm, travels into the past and becomes involved in the lives of the Babington family, who had once owned it. Her special friend in this fascinating sixteenth century world where Elizabeth 1st reigns, is young Francis Babington, and when with him she discovers Anthony Babington's devotion to Mary Queen of Scots, imprisoned at neighbouring Wingfield Manor, she tries to warn Anthony of his peril. For she can remember from her 20th century life the tragedies that occurred to those who supported the exiled Queen, but she cannot explain to the Babingtons how she comes by her knowledge, so is forced to watch while events take their inevitable course.

Willie the Squowse

Ted Allan

Back to back in a city there were two old houses. In one
lived the Pickerings, a charming old couple, in the other the
squealing, quarrelsome Smiths – and in the wall between
the two houses, Willie the Squowse. Willie was unusual,
half squirrel, half mouse, and clever as a cartload of
monkeys.

He did look a bit like a mouse, so he knew the Pickerings
and the Smiths wouldn't welcome him, but he'd be safe
if he kept out of sight. The only problem was the delicious
cheese which Mrs Smith placed so tantalisingly close to his
hole, but Willie was clever enough to deal with that – he'd
block out the dangerously tempting smell with some of
those crisp new pieces of paper that Mrs Pickering hid
in her side of the wall each week with such smiles of
satisfaction, although in the five years he daily plugged the
hole he never understood just what those bits of paper
were.

Carbonel and Calidor

Barbara Sleigh

'You do look a Charlie!' said John when Rosemary tried on
the paper hat, but Rosemary didn't feel like laughing. She
felt strangely solemn. Then she tried on the ring which had
fallen from the cracker, and she thought she heard a voice
say, 'Help, John and Rosemary,' but it was later that she
discovered their old friend Carbonel, King of the
Fallowhithe Cats, needed their help to search for his
runaway son, Prince Calidor, and that the flashing red
ring had turned her and John into Hearing Humans, who
could understand the language of animals.

Ned Kelly and the City of the Bees

Thomas Keneally

What would you do if you were lying in a hospital bed
waiting to have your appendix taken out, and a
sympathetic bee offered you the chance of visiting her
hive? Ned Kelly didn't hesitate for long. Luckily, he had
Miss Nancy Clancy to show him round, and as she'd been
living in the hive for more than a hundred years she knew
it pretty well.

Ned hadn't meant to stay a whole summer with the bees
but he hung on to find out what would happen next.
Would the revolt the drones were planning for the autumn
be successful? Was the Queen growing too old? If so,
who would be her successor? With questions like these it
would be hard for Ned to tear himself away.

Runaway Ralph

Beverly Cleary

Ralph was the only mouse in the Mountain View Inn who
owned a motorcycle. It was a gorgeous red one, just the
right size for a mouse, and he rode it up and down the
hall at nights like a perfect daredevil. It was bliss on that
motorbike, and Ralph would have stayed there riding it
forever, if it hadn't been for his aunts and uncles shaking
their heads over the waste of time, and all his silly little
cousins clamouring for pushes on the bike as if it were a toy.

So Ralph made a great decision. He left home that very
night, coasting happily downhill to the Happy Acres
Summer Camp for Boys and Girls, a place his dreams told
him would be full of freedom and peanut-butter-and-jelly
sandwiches. How sad it was that the reality was so
unspeakably terrifying that even the Mountain View Inn
and the tedious little cousins were attractive by
comparison!

Heard about the Puffin Club?

... it's a way of finding out more about Puffin books and authors, of winning prizes (in competitions), sharing jokes, a secret code, and perhaps seeing your name in print! When you join you get a copy of our magazine, *Puffin Post*, sent to you four times a year, a badge and a membership book.

For details of subscription and an application form, send a stamped addressed envelope to:

The Puffin Club Dept A
Penguin Books Limited
Bath Road
Harmondsworth
Middlesex UB7 ODA

and if you live in Australia, please write to:

The Australian Puffin Club
Penguin Books Australia Limited
P.O. Box 257
Ringwood
Victoria 3134